HERE TODAY

HERE

TODAY

Ann M. Martin

SCHOLASTIC PRESS / NEW YORK

Copyright © 2004 by Ann M. Martin.

All rights reserved. Published by Scholastic Press, an imprint of Scholastic Inc., *Publishers since 1920.*

SCHOLASTIC, SCHOLASTIC PRESS, and associated logos are trademarks and/or registered trademarks of Scholastic Inc.

Library of Congress Cataloging-in-Publication Data

Here today / Ann M. Martin.—1st ed.   p. cm.

Summary: In 1963, when her flamboyant mother abandons the family to pursue her dreams of becoming an actress, eleven-year-old Ellie Dingman takes charge of her younger siblings, while also trying to deal with the outcast status in school and frightening acts of prejudice toward the "misfits" that live on her street.

ISBN 0-439-57944-9 (alk. paper)

[1. Identity—Fiction.   2. Mothers—Fiction.   3. Family life—New York (State)—Fiction.
4. Prejudices—Fiction.   5. Neighborhood—Fiction.   6. Schools—Fiction.   7. New York (State)—
History—20th century—Fiction.]   I. Title.

PZ7.M3567585Her 2004   [Fic]—dc22   2004041620

10 9 8 7 6 5 4 3 2 1   ·   04 05 06 07 08

The text type was set in Pastonchi   ·   Book design by Elizabeth B. Parisi

First edition, October 2004

For Liz Szabla

PART ONE

The Bosetti Beauty

In 1963. Ellie's mother. Doris Day Dingman, was crowned the Bosetti Beauty at Mr. Bosetti's supermarket. President John F. Kennedy was assassinated, and the Dingmans began to fall apart. Most of this happened in the second part of the year — a year that had gotten off to a pretty good start, considering they were the Dingmans.

Ellie and Doris were downtown shopping with her mother when they first saw the contest sign in the window of Mr. Bosetti's store.

"Eleanor! Will you look at that!" exclaimed Doris.

Doris was proud of the names she had given her children: Eleanor Roosevelt, Albert Einstein, and Marie Curie. Most people called Albert and Marie Albert and Marie, but they shortened Eleanor to Ellie. Not Doris, though. Eleanor had been named after the wife of a president of the United States, and Doris did not want to take away from that.

It was a blistering hot day in the middle of August. Ellie, standing on the sidewalk in downtown Spectacle, felt waves of heat rise up out of the pavement and engulf her navy Keds and bare legs. She was scratching the back of her right calf with the toe of her left sneaker when Doris pointed a long, red-painted fingernail at a sign in Bosetti's window. It read:

FREE FOOD!
ENTER OUR DRAWING
AND WIN
A 5-MINUTE SHOPPING SPREE!
DETAILS INSIDE

"Come on," Doris said, grabbing Ellie's hand and heading for the door. "I have *got* to enter that."

"But Doris, we don't shop here." The Dingmans shopped at the A&P, which was much cheaper. "Aren't you supposed to shop at Bosetti's to be eligible to enter their contest?"

Doris smiled, pleased with the big word Ellie had used. But she replied, "The sign doesn't say anything about shopping here. I have a right to enter the contest. And we could use that free food more than any of the people who do shop here."

Doris swung open the door to Bosetti's, pulling Ellie behind her, and swept inside. She liked to make entrances.

Ellie looked around at the shelves and displays. Bosetti's carried items such as little wrinkly mushrooms, tinned oysters, and pomegranates. What the Dingmans needed were Kleenex and Wonder bread, but once Doris got an idea in her head, it was hard to shake it loose.

"Where do I sign up for the contest?" Doris asked a cashier.

"Right over there." The woman indicated a fish bowl sitting on a wooden table. Next to the bowl was a stack of entry blanks and a ballpoint pen. "Just fill out a form."

"Thanks," said Doris. She scribbled her name and address on a blank and dropped it in the bowl.

"Okay. Great. Let's go," Ellie whispered, and rushed toward the door.

Doris didn't pay any attention to her. She was filling out a second form.

"Doris, that's cheating!" Ellie returned to Doris's side, taking note of the other shoppers in Bosetti's and feeling grateful that she didn't recognize any of them.

"Hush." Doris elbowed Ellie. "The sign didn't say anything about how many to fill out, either."

"No, but the lady did. She said fill out a form. *A* form."

"Hush," said Doris again. "That's just a matter of speech, or whatever you call it. Now let me concentrate."

"Jackie Kennedy wouldn't cheat," muttered Ellie, but Doris didn't hear her.

3

Doris filled out exactly twenty-five blanks while Ellie squirmed and blushed and kept checking on the cashier to see if she was watching, but she wasn't.

One week later, when Doris got a phone call saying she had won the contest at Bosetti's, she screamed and jumped up and down like she had only filled out one form and had been lucky. But as she said to Ellie and Albert and Marie, "If you want to get anywhere in this world, you have to take matters into your own hands, and then be a little bit lucky."

The contest was to be held on Monday, August 26. That morning, the Dingman children crowded into their parents' bedroom to watch Doris get ready. They were allowed to watch her makeup and wardrobe process from the underwear point on. Doris would emerge from the bathroom wearing her bra and slip and stockings, and seat herself at the dressing table in the bedroom — the bedroom that was much more hers than Mr. Dingman's.

Ellie, Albert, and Marie lay in a sweaty row across the bed, Ellie and Albert on the ends, Marie in the middle. They rested their chins in their hands and watched. Doris was the prettiest woman in Spectacle, New York. This wasn't just what she believed. It was actually true. There was not another lady like her.

Which was how Doris had gotten to do things like be the Lehman's Spam Spread Girl outside the A&P, and play all the princess roles in the community theater productions.

"For a proper beehive," Doris was now saying as she teased her hair into a teetering heap on top of her head, "you need both VO5 *and* combs."

Marie watched in fascination, mouth open, breathing heavily.

"What's your color scheme going to be?" asked Albert.

There was always a color scheme, and it was always loud.

"Blue and orange," Doris answered promptly. She indicated the dress hanging on the outside of the closet door. "Mr. Howard Johnson knew what he was doing, that's for sure."

Half an hour later, Doris was finished. She examined herself in the mirror: bright blue combs in the beehive, orange glasses (the ones with the rhinestones at the corners), electrifying blue dress with orange patent-leather belt cinched very tight at the waist, and blue sneakers, which she needed in order to turn tight corners and be as speedy as possible in Bosetti's.

Marie gazed at her rapturously. "You look like a Popsicle!"

"Thanks, hon," Doris replied vaguely. She smoothed the skirt of her dress as she stood up. "Well," she said, "I wish your father could be here to see this."

Mr. Dingman couldn't take a morning off to watch Doris run around Bosetti's. He was grateful for every bit of work he got. Construction jobs dried up in the winter, so he took advantage of the summer ones.

"All right, kids. Off we go," said Doris.

"Holly's coming with us, okay?" Ellie said as she ran downstairs.

"The more the merrier," said Doris.

Ellie dashed across Witch Tree Lane and yelled to Holly from the Majors' front stoop. Holly must have been waiting, because her front door flew open immediately. Moments later she and Ellie were in the backseat of the Dingmans' Buick, and Doris was driving, at an alarming pace, toward downtown Spectacle.

"Look at all the back-to-school signs," said Albert, groaning, when they reached King Street. "I don't want to go back to school."

"You're smart," said Doris, who was searching for a parking space. "You have a good brain. Be thankful."

"I am," said Albert, "but I still don't like school."

Neither did Ellie. Or Holly or Marie. School was not a pleasant place for a Witch Tree Lane kid.

Albert crossed his arms and kicked his sneakers against the back of the front seat, leaving dusty scuff marks.

"Will you look at all these people!" exclaimed Doris. "I've never *seen* downtown so crowded."

Ellie, her window wide open so the hot breeze could blow her damp hair out of her face, didn't think Spectacle looked any more crowded than it usually did on a weekday at the end of summer. It wasn't a large town like Utica. And it certainly wasn't a city like Manhattan, which Doris longed to visit one day. But it wasn't a tiny town, either. It was big enough to have a hospital and a library, two movie theaters, and four churches. It even had its own high school. Spectacle kids didn't have to travel to Central High like the kids in the surrounding towns did. And on King Street, the main street, there were plenty of shops and businesses, six restaurants (including La Duchesse Anne, which was French and served snails and crepes), and two diners.

Doris nosed the Buick around a corner and pulled into the parking lot behind the dry cleaner's. Ellie and Holly glanced at each other, relieved. Doris was a horrible parallel parker, jerking the car forward and back, slamming on the brakes, waving other drivers around her with frantic gestures, and occasionally swearing. Ellie privately thought that Doris liked the small audience she attracted, and was grateful each time Doris opted to park in a lot.

"All right, kids," said Doris as they climbed out of the car and walked back to King Street. "I don't know if you're allowed in the store with me during the contest. It's not very big in there and I'll need room to maneuver the cart. So just stay together outside."

"Okay," said Ellie and Albert and Holly.

"Can't I come with you, Doris?" asked Marie. "Please?"

"What did I just say, Marie? You stick with Eleanor." Doris tried to pat Marie's head, but Marie ducked out of her reach. "Oh, my God!" exclaimed Doris as they neared Bosetti's. "That's a bigger crowd than I expected. Mr. Bosetti must have done some advanced publicity."

"Ad*vance*," said Ellie under her breath.

"I'm so nervous," said Doris, who didn't look nervous at all.

Ellie considered the crowd. It was bigger than she had expected, too. She didn't really see what was so interesting about watching someone careen through a store with a shopping cart. On the other hand, it was Doris who would be careening through the store with the cart, and Spectaculars, as Ellie thought of the citizens of Spectacle, nearly always turned out to watch Doris.

"All right. Off I go!" Doris ran ahead, made her way to the entrance to Bosetti's, waved to the crowd, and hurried inside.

Holly and the Dingman children stood at the edge of the crowd.

"We have to get to the front," said Albert. "We'll never be able to see from back here."

"I don't want to go to the front," Holly whispered to Ellie. "Everyone will stare at us."

"I don't want to go, either," Ellie replied, "but Doris will be really disappointed if she finds out we didn't see her. It's bad enough that Dad isn't here. Come on."

Ellie took Marie's hand and began to edge through the crowd. Albert and Holly followed. They ducked under elbows and squeezed by shopping bags. "Sorry. I'm sorry," said Ellie over and over again.

When they reached Bosetti's window, Marie stood on her tiptoes. "I can't see," she said automatically.

"Yes, you can. It's a great view," Ellie told her. "Just look inside." The window was large, and Mr. Bosetti had taken down all the signs for marzipan and olives and imported cheeses that were usually posted in it. "See? There's Doris."

On the other side of the window Doris was poised with an empty shopping cart. Even though Mr. Bosetti was still talking to her, giving her last-minute instructions,

Doris had assumed a runner's stance, balanced on the balls of her feet, ready to take off.

From behind her Ellie heard snickering and soft laughter.

Albert whirled around.

"Don't," said Ellie. "Forget them." She faced Albert forward. "Anyway, not everyone is laughing."

Mr. Bosetti left Doris with her cart and appeared in the door to his store. "Let's have a countdown," he said to Doris's audience. He raised one hand in the air, then lowered it. "Ten!" he cried. He raised his hand again, and the crowd began to count with him. "Nine! Eight! Seven, six, five, four, three, two . . . ONE!"

Doris shoved the cart forward and flew down the nearest aisle, grabbing items off the shelves as she went.

"She's not even looking," said Albert. "What do we want with anchovies?"

"How much time does she have?" asked Holly.

"Five minutes," said Ellie.

Doris sailed to the end of the aisle and swung the cart around so fast that it nearly tipped over.

"Oh, my," a woman said, and let out a snort of laughter. She turned to the woman standing next to her and whispered something. Ellie watched them, their heads bent together, hair swinging, their bare arms linked. They were Doris's age, Ellie guessed. They were thirty-one, at least, but when Ellie looked at them she saw Maggie Paxton and Nancy Becker from last year, from fifth grade.

"Hush," said the second woman as she tried to stifle her laughter.

"I can't help it," said the first one. "She's just so . . . so *cheap*."

Ellie took a step backward. She decided to concentrate on the clock inside Bosetti's.

"How many more minutes?" asked Marie when Doris reached the produce aisle.

"Two," Ellie said, and pulled herself up stiffly as she heard a male voice say, "Got quite a wiggle, don't she?"

Face burning, Ellie trained her eyes on the window, but shut out Doris, Mr. Bosetti, the store, the laughter, Marie tugging at her hand. She willed herself to her private place, the one she could summon when she needed an escape — and was only jerked away from it when she heard Holly draw her breath in sharply.

Ellie refocused her eyes in time to see Doris try to balance an enormous canned ham on top of the pile in her cart, then lunge forward as the ham teetered and slid toward the floor.

"Time!" shouted Mr. Bosetti as the ham crashed to the linoleum.

Doris looked at her cart, at Mr. Bosetti, at the ham on the floor. "Can I keep it?" she asked sheepishly.

"Sure, why not?" Mr. Bosetti was leading Doris toward the front door. "After all, you, Doris Day Dingman, have just become . . . our first Bosetti Beauty!"

"Their first what?" Holly said to Ellie, her voice raised so Ellie could hear her over the noise of the crowd.

"Your Bosetti Beauty?" repeated Doris.

Grinning, Mr. Bosetti reached for a rhinestone-studded tiara and pressed it into Doris's beehive. "Ladies and gentlemen, inspired by the lovely Doris Dingman, I have decided to crown a Bosetti Beauty every year. But we will always remember Doris as our first. Congratulations!"

Doris turned a beaming face to the crowd. "Thank you, thank you!" she said. "And I want to thank my husband and children. My husband couldn't be here today, but my children —"

Mr. Bosetti stepped in front of Doris. "Please think of Bosetti's when you think of fine food," he said to the crowd. "Our store will reopen in fifteen minutes. Don't go far!" He steered Doris back inside.

Twenty minutes later, Holly and the Dingmans were driving home with the overflowing bags from Bosetti's. Doris's tiara was in place.

"This has been a morning to remember," she said breathlessly.

Witch Tree Lane

To get to Witch Tree Lane, which was actually a cul-de-sac, you had to drive almost out of Spectacle and take the last turnoff from Route 27 before Pious, six miles to the west. Every time Ellie neared her street she was struck by two opposing feelings, and wasn't sure how her heart had room for both of them. She felt a tugging fondness for her small house and the four other houses on the street. And she felt a pang of embarrassment at being one of the people who lived on Witch Tree Lane. For the truth was, although Ellie loved her family and her neighbors dearly, there wasn't a single normal person on Witch Tree Lane, at least in the eyes of Spectaculars.

There were the Majors, Holly and her mother. Holly called her mother Mom, but most people in Spectacle called her Selena because they weren't certain what else to call her. They couldn't call her Mrs. Major since she *wasn't married* (Major was Selena's last name, not Holly's father's). And "Miss Major" sounded like the name on the envelope for an invitation to a child's birthday party. So people settled on Selena. Selena had become a mother when she was sixteen years old, which was a full four years earlier than Doris had first become a mother. And she had never shown any interest in providing Holly with a father. Most people, including Holly, didn't even know who her father was.

Next door to the Majors lived the Lauchaires. The Lauchaires were *foreign*, or at least partly so. They had moved to Spectacle from Belgium, and everybody spoke French. But Mrs. Lauchaire, who worked as a temporary secretary, was originally from Pious. And Etienne, who was nine years old and Albert's best friend, and Dominique, who was seven and one of Marie's best friends, spoke English unless they were at home. At home they had to speak French because their father, Monsieur Lauchaire, had never learned how to speak English, which explained why he had found his silent, solitary job with the maintenance crew at the community college. As if all this weren't enough, the Lauchaires were messy. Their house was a mess, the kids were a mess, their yard was a mess. Ellie thought they were wonderful.

Across the street from the Lauchaires and next door to the Dingmans was the Levins' house. The Levins were not foreign, but they were from Brooklyn, which was part of New York City — and they were bohemian.

Also, they were Jewish. They went to temple twelve miles away in Sharonville, which was where the nearest synagogue was. And the Levin children — David, who was eleven like Ellie and Holly, Rachel, who was eight and friends with Domi Lauchaire and Marie, and Allan, who was six and the youngest kid on the street — went to Hebrew school in addition to Washington Irving Elementary. Mr. and Mrs. Levin had left Brooklyn because they didn't want to raise their kids in the city, and had moved to Spectacle and settled into their small house with teaching jobs at the same community college where Monsieur Lauchaire mopped the floors and weeded the gardens. The three Levin kids went barefoot all summer, Mr. Levin had let his hair grow long, and Mrs. Levin wore embroidered peasant blouses *without a bra*.

The fifth house on Witch Tree Lane was the oldest. It was situated at the very end of the cul-de-sac, so that from the front porch you could look straight past the four other houses to the intersection of the lane with Route 27. Two elderly ladies lived in this house — two ladies who had lived together for years and were *not related*. Miss Nelson and Miss Woods. Ellie and the eight other children on Witch Tree Lane thought of them as their grandmothers. The ladies were usually at home, unlike the children's parents, all of whom worked at least part-time (except for Doris, but she was rarely home, anyway). Miss Nelson and Miss Woods were good at tending things. They pottered around in their gardens, and gladly stirred up batches of lemonade for the children, bandaged scraped elbows, and occasionally helped out with tough homework assignments.

Also, they took care of the Witch Tree for which the street had been named. It was an oak at the edge of their property, near the Levins' yard, and was huge and ancient and misunderstood. A large knothole several feet above the ground was shaped vaguely like the profile of an old woman with a very long nose and a very pointy chin, and even the suggestion of an eye. Spectaculars were afraid of the tree, and believed it possessed supernatural powers. Which only added to their long list of suspicions about Witch Tree Lane and the people who lived there.

None of this was fair, Ellie thought, including the fact that a face with a long nose and a pointy chin should be considered witchy. Plenty of nonwitches had long noses and pointy chins. And real witches could probably look like anything. After all, Glinda the Good Witch of the North in *The Wizard of Oz* was young and beautiful, with a short nose and a little round chin. But the Witch Tree was the Witch Tree and that was that.

It was as much a Spectacular outcast as the people who lived on the street.

As Doris wheeled the Buick and its cargo of children and fine foods off of Route 27, Ellie greeted the sight of Witch Tree Lane with her mixed pangs of love and shame.

"Home again, home again," said Doris.

After a brief silence, Marie said sullenly, "Jiggity-jig." She was still mad about not having been allowed inside Bosetti's with Doris.

Albert hopped out of the car. "Going to Etienne's," he said as he slammed the door.

"I'm going with you," said Marie.

Kiss, the Dingmans' dog, jumped up from a spot of shade by the garage, licked Ellie exuberantly, then ran after Albert and Marie.

"Eleanor, Holly, help me with the food," said Doris, who then hurried inside, leaving the food-putting-away to the girls.

"Look at her. She just disappears," said Ellie crossly.

"Oh, well," replied Holly, which she said all the time, and which Ellie found comforting.

Doris reappeared in time for lunch, still wearing the tiara and her Bosetti's outfit. "Come on, we can have a cocktail party," she said. "Finger foods and hors d'oeuvres and all. I bet this is what Jackie Kennedy serves when she and the president give a White House party for state heads and royal people."

Holly stayed for lunch and she and Doris and Ellie ate tiny wieners and sesame crackers and slices of avocado. They sampled spicy mustard and a jar of something called Snappies.

"Marzipan for dessert?" asked Ellie.

But Holly said she ought to go home. "I promised Mom I'd practice piano this afternoon. And clean the bathroom. Come over later, though, okay?"

"Sure," said Ellie. She would be there in time for a *Mickey Mouse Club* rerun. Although she and Holly claimed to be too old for the show, they secretly enjoyed it, in the same way they sometimes secretly talked to their old Barbies, so they were relieved that Marie and Rachel always wanted to watch. Also, Ellie and Holly had crushes on Jimmie Dodd, the very cute host of the show. Holly spent hours imagining that he was her boyfriend.

Holly left, and Ellie and Doris sat in the Dingmans' humid, dimly lit kitchen. Albert and Marie hadn't reappeared. Ellie wasn't used to having Doris at home and all to herself. "Doris?" she said. "What are you going to do this afternoon?"

Doris spent most of her free time at classes — voice and tap dance and elocution and comportment. "It's important to build up your résumé," she told Ellie. Ellie had heard a lot about Doris's résumé, but had never seen it. All she knew was that every time there was an opportunity for Doris to sing or dance or act in Spectacle, off she rushed, bragging about her résumé. "I've got more talent in my little finger than anyone in Spectacle," she would tell Ellie.

There weren't many such opportunities, though, so during all the lulls, Doris created opportunities for herself. For instance, it was Doris who had talked the A&P people into letting her be the Lehman's Spam Spread Girl. "In this world, Eleanor, you have to make things happen. You can't just sit around waiting."

This was, in fact, the reason Doris, who had been born with the perfectly good name of Darlene Larsen (which had become Darlene Dingman when she married Ellie's father), had changed her name to Doris Day.

"I had to jump-start my show business career," she told Ellie.

"But why did you choose Doris Day? That name's already taken."

"Well, of course it is. That's the point. I need the name to call attention to myself. Once I get a big movie role, I'll change my name again. Doris Day isn't Doris

Day's real name, after all. This is part of show business, Eleanor."

Doris looked at Ellie now over the kitchen table, which was littered with wrappers and peels and seeds. "I think I'll work on my suntan," she said. She cocked her head. "Do you think Jackie goes sunbathing behind the White House? God, she's lucky. Young and beautiful and always in the magazines. Of course, I don't know that she's particularly talented. But look where looks and glamour have gotten her." She paused. "Do you?"

"Do I what?" said Ellie.

"Do you think she goes sunbathing?"

"Jackie Kennedy? Gosh, Doris, I don't know. Maybe. Probably not at the White House, though. People would see her. I don't think it's very private there. Maybe she sunbathes when they go to their beach."

"Oh, of course," said Doris dreamily. "All right, hon. I'm going to put on my bathing suit. Keep me company?"

The Dingmans' backyard was tiny. And while it was more private than the White House, it was still bordered by Route 27 on one side and the Levins' house on the other. This didn't prevent Doris from lathering herself with a mixture of baby oil and iodine and lying on a lounge chair in her two-piece suit. Truckers on Route 27 blasted their horns at her as they whirred by, and once in a while a car full of boys would slow down and the boys would lean out the windows and whistle. Doris waved gaily to the truckers and the boys while Ellie huddled in a deck chair. She refused to wear a bathing suit, had even changed from her shorts into pants, although she was now boiling. When you were a Witch Tree Lane kid, you called as little attention to yourself as possible. Ellie, who was intrigued by the notion of camouflage, had read and reread an entire book on chameleons. She and Kiss now sat on a blue deck chair, Ellie wearing a blue T-shirt, blue dungarees, and a blue sun hat. She had pulled the deck chair up to the back wall of the house so that she had to yell to talk with Doris.

"Doris? Do you want a book or something?" she called. Ellie was getting bored. She couldn't understand how her mother could just lie in the yard for hours on end.

"No thanks. Come talk to me, Eleanor."

"I'm good over here."

"But I want to talk to you."

Ellie heaved a sigh. "Okay." She dragged her chair closer to Doris, but not so close that she could be easily noticed from the road. Kiss followed her.

"So, hon, school's about to start again," said Doris to the sky. She lay rigidly on her back, determined to get an even tan.

"Yup," replied Ellie.

"And?"

"And what?"

"Don't you remember what we talked about? How this is going to be your year?"

Ellie heaved another sigh. *Doris* had talked about this. Ellie had only listened to her, and she had not agreed to anything.

"I think it's *your* year, Doris," said Ellie. "You got to do your recitation in the talent show and now you're the Bosetti Beauty." She leaned down to scratch Kiss's ears.

"I have lots more plans, too," said Doris, brightening. "First off, I'm going to approach Harwell's about a fashion show."

"Harwell's? The department store?" The Dingmans couldn't afford to shop at Harwell's, with its tiny, tasteful boutiques (Misses, Juniors, Little Girls, Matrons — which meant large women — The Gentleman's Corner, Cruise Wear) and its discreet dressing rooms. Ellie's clothes came from the bulging racks at Korvette's, which didn't even have dressing rooms.

"I've seen the new fall fashions," said Doris, "and what Harwell's needs is someone to model them."

"But you've never been a model," said Ellie.

"Well, I have to start somewhere. And I've taken all those classes. I know how to do my own makeup and walk gracefully and comport myself. Put me in the right outfit and I'll look just like — like —"

"Jackie Kennedy?" suggested Ellie. "Doris Day? Grace Kelly?"

"Yes! Any one of them. Harwell's will jump at the chance." Doris studied Ellie. "So? What about you? What are you going to do this year? Why don't you try out for something?"

"Well," said Ellie, "maybe."

"I know you. 'Maybe' means 'no.'"

Ellie shrugged.

"Take up an instrument for the school band. You've got to do something to stand out."

"I think I'm going to have a lot of homework," said Ellie vaguely. She stretched. "Doris, I have to go. It's almost time for *The Mickey Mouse Club*. I'll see you later."

Ellie and Holly watched the show, joined by Albert, Marie, Rachel, Kiss, and Pumpkin, Holly's orange tabby cat. Marie, Rachel, and Kiss wore caps with Mickey Mouse ears on them. When the show was over — when the Mouseketeers had sung the sad song about saying good-bye to their company — the sun was in the west, and the shadows on Witch Tree Lane were lengthening. Ellie looked out the Majors' front window and saw her father's truck in their driveway.

"Come on," she said to Albert and Marie. "Dad's home."

Ellie found her father rummaging around in the refrigerator. He was sweaty and sawdusty, his fingers grimy, his clothes smelling faintly of turpentine.

"Hi, sweetie," said Mr. Dingman, kissing the top of Ellie's head. "Where's your mother?"

Ellie pointed out the window to the yard where Doris was soaking up the last rays of the afternoon sun. Then she looked at Marie leaning against the kitchen counter, still wearing her Mickey Mouse ears. "Go tell Doris that Dad's here," she said to her. "I guess I'll start supper," she added.

The Bump in the Road

In 1964, after the Dingmans had fallen apart, Ellie thought she should be able to look back at 1963 and see when things had started to go wrong. She knew that falling apart had been a long, slow process, one that in truth had started before she'd been born; probably even before her father and Doris had met each other. Still, she thought that it was sometime after the morning at Bosetti's that her family encountered the first real bump in the road.

Ellie's mind settled on the day Doris had driven downtown to her meeting with the Harwell's people. It was a day that had dawned sticky and hot and threatened rain. All morning long the people in Spectacle had waited for the rain. By early afternoon Miss Nelson and Miss Woods sat on their front porch cooling themselves with fans they had made by folding pages from magazines back and forth, back and forth, into accordions.

"Hotter than the hinges of Hades," commented Miss Nelson.

"Can I make a fan, too?" asked Domi Lauchaire.

"And me?" asked Marie.

Six of the Witch Tree Lane kids — Domi, Marie, Ellie, Holly, Rachel, and Allan — were crowded onto the ladies' front porch, along with Kiss and Pumpkin. Etienne, Albert, and David were at the Lauchaires' building a G.I. Joe fort. All of their parents were at work, except for Doris, who was at Harwell's.

Miss Nelson disappeared inside the little house and returned with a copy of *Good Housekeeping* and a stapler. "Now here," she said. "Come watch. I'll show you what to do." She demonstrated selecting an appealing page from the magazine (preferably one with flowers or an animal on it), carefully tearing it out, then folding the accordion pleats, and finally stapling them together at one end.

"Ahh," said Miss Nelson, fanning her face and neck.

The younger children pounced on the magazine.

"Roses!" exclaimed Rachel triumphantly, holding up an ad for room deodorizer.

"Let me see!" cried Marie. "I want to look for a picture of a dog like Kiss."

"Well, let Rachel tear out her page first," said Miss Woods. Then she glanced at Kiss, a black-and-brown mutt who wasn't bad looking, she thought, except for her unfortunate underbite, and added, "I'm not sure,

Marie, that you'll be able to find a picture of a dog *exactly* like Kiss."

"Yes, I will. Yes, I will," said Marie, who, lately, had become more and more stubborn.

The kids pored over the magazine and fumbled with their folding and stapling. Miss Woods made a pitcher of lemonade, and the early part of the afternoon passed slowly.

Still, the rain didn't come.

Miss Nelson announced that she needed to go to the grocery store, and drove off in Millie, the ladies' blue truck.

Next door, Albert, Etienne, and David exited the Lauchaires' carrying a large cardboard box.

"What's that?" cried Allan. He had been sitting on the edge of the porch, bare legs hanging over the side. Now he jumped to his feet.

"It's our fort," replied Etienne. He set the box down in the grass, and the children on the porch ran to it and peeked inside.

"Here's the army headquarters," explained Albert.

"And that's where they hide tanks and bombs," added David.

"Neat," said Allan, but since everything in the box was imaginary, except for two G.I. Joes, the children soon lost interest and drifted away.

"I'm bored, Ellie," said Domi.

"Me, too," said Marie.

They looked at Ellie expectantly.

"Well," she said after a moment.

"Make up a game! Make up a game!" chanted Rachel.

The Witch Tree Lane kids crowded around Ellie, waiting. In the past, on hot, slow days such as this one, Ellie had been responsible for inventing Pig Tag, Who's the Strangest?, Ambulance Rescue, and Naughty, Naughty Baby.

"How about Ambulance Rescue?" suggested Ellie.

"No, no, it has to be a new one!" said Etienne.

"All right," said Ellie slowly. "How about, let me see . . . how about Naked Barbie Football?"

The boys hooted, the girls giggled, and Domi fell to the ground. "I faint with excitement," she exclaimed.

"How do you play Naked Barbie Football?" asked Holly.

"Well, first everyone has to go get their Barbies," said Ellie. "We need as many as possible. And when you find them, take off their clothes. We only want naked Barbies."

"Should we bring Kens, too?" asked Marie. "Or just Barbies?"

"Barbies only," said Ellie decisively. "Okay, everyone. Go to your houses, find the Barbies, undress them, and bring them back here."

"Do you need footballs for this game?" asked David.

"Um, no," replied Ellie, who, so far, had no idea how the game would be played.

Ten minutes later the Witch Tree Lane kids gathered again in the Lauchaires' yard. And once again they looked expectantly at Ellie.

"First," said Ellie, "count the Barbies. Do we have enough for a football team?"

The children had just laid the Barbies on the grass to count them when two things happened at once. Domi shrieked, "Mommy's home!" as a car turned into the Lauchaires' driveway. And the first drops of rain started to fall. Ellie heard the rumble of thunder.

"Domi! Etienne!" called Mrs. Lauchaire. "Come on inside."

Lightning flashed, and the kids scattered to their homes, Holly scooping up Pumpkin as she ran. By the time Ellie, Albert, Marie, and Kiss reached their front door, they were damp. And Kiss was trembling at the sound of the thunder, her tail between her legs. She squeezed past the kids as Ellie opened the door, flew into the living room, and tunneled behind the couch.

Albert and Marie sat on the back of the couch, which was under the picture window, and watched the storm on their street. They watched as the rain blew against the panes of glass; as Miss Nelson returned in Millie, wipers going at a furious speed; as the wind picked up a newspaper and sent it sailing down the lane where it wrapped itself wetly around the Witch Tree; and as one by one the parents came home from work.

By five-thirty all the parents on the street were home except for Doris.

"Where's your mother?" Mr. Dingman asked Ellie as he stood dripping in the kitchen, wiping his head and face with a dish towel.

It was a perfectly absolutely ordinary moment, and yet, Ellie realized later, it was that first bump in the road.

Ellie was about to reply, "She went to Harwell's," when she felt someone staring at her from behind. Uneasy, she turned away from her father, turned toward the kitchen door, and there was Albert, a naked Barbie in his hand, still perched on the back of the couch, but now facing the other way, staring into the kitchen at Ellie and Mr. Dingman.

"Yeah, where is she?" said Albert.

"You know where she is. She went to Harwell's," Ellie replied.

"She's shopping at Harwell's?" Mr. Dingman asked, his voice rising to a higher pitch.

"No, no. She's not shopping there," Ellie said quickly, turning back to her father. "She just went for a meeting. About the fashion show."

Mr. Dingman folded the dish towel carefully and placed it on the table so that the edge of the cloth and the edge of the table were lined up exactly. "What fashion show?" he asked.

"The one Doris is going to star in," said Marie. She crawled behind the couch and attempted to pull Kiss out, but Kiss wouldn't budge.

Ellie's father slid a chair out from under the kitchen table and very slowly sat down on it.

"Dad, I think Doris told you about this," said Ellie.

Before Mr. Dingman could answer, Albert said, "She's been gone for hours. Meetings don't take that long." He slid off of the couch and walked stiffly into the kitchen.

"How do you know how long fashion show meetings take?" asked Marie.

Albert ignored her. "She left at quarter after one," he reported. He glanced at the clock in the kitchen. "Now it's twenty to six."

"I'm hungry," said Marie.

"I'll start dinner," said Ellie.

"Doris should start dinner," said Albert. He stood in the middle of the room, feet apart, slamming his right fist into his left hand, over and over again.

"Well, she can't now, can she?" said Ellie sharply. "Besides, I make dinner all the time."

"That's different. It's different when you're just helping her out."

"Kids." Mr. Dingman rested his head in his hands. "Just . . . be quiet for a minute."

No one said anything.

"Shouldn't I start dinner?" Ellie finally asked.

"I guess so," said her father.

"I'm really starving," said Marie.

"I just said I'll start dinner," snapped Ellie.

"How long are we going to wait for Doris?" asked Albert, crossing his arms.

Ellie removed two pots from the cabinet next to the sink and banged them onto the counter. She found a box of rice and banged it down next to the pots.

Mr. Dingman sat silently, gazing out at the storm.

"I *said*, 'How long are we going to wait for Doris?'" Albert still stood in the middle of the room, arms crossed.

"Everybody heard you," said Ellie.

"No one answered me."

"I want Doris," said Marie, setting up to wail.

"Well, she's not here," said Albert. "As usual."

Mr. Dingman spun around in his chair. "Albert, that's enough."

"But —"

"Enough!"

"She's supposed to be here," persisted Albert, and his voice shook slightly. "All the other mothers came home. I saw them."

"I want Doris!" cried Marie.

Ellie looked at her father. After what seemed like a very long time, he rose from his chair, examined the grit embedded in his fingertips, then flung his hands to his sides as if the dirt were a tough problem he'd have to address later. "Marie, help your sister," he snapped. "Albert, come with me."

"No."

"We need to talk."

"No."

"Albert, come with me this *instant*." Mr. Dingman's voice was rising. *"Right. Now."* He took a step toward Albert.

"Daddy!" Marie wailed.

"NO!" Albert ran from the kitchen and up the stairs to his room, where he slammed the door shut.

Mr. Dingman strode out of the kitchen. Ellie heard him run up the stairs, heard him rap sharply on Albert's door.

"Set the table, Marie," said Ellie, hating herself for sounding crabby.

Sniffling, Marie headed for the cutlery drawer.

"Wash your hands first."

"You're not the boss of me."

"Just do it. Please."

Marie washed her hands, then set the kitchen table. Four places.

Twenty minutes later, Ellie's dinner of rice and hot dogs and Green Giant canned peas was ready. Albert and Mr. Dingman came back downstairs, and the Dingmans ate silently.

It was after nine o'clock that night when the front door banged open. Marie was already upstairs asleep, but Ellie, Albert, and Mr. Dingman were watching TV. Albert kept his eyes glued to the set.

"Yoo-hoo!" called Doris as she walked unsteadily into the living room.

"Doris," said Mr. Dingman. "You're — for heaven's sake, the children."

"Oh, now, don't start. Don't ruin it for me. Just let me be excited about this."

"But —"

"Well, I had to go out and celebrate. Didn't I? I think they're going to say yes."

Albert slid off the couch and edged toward the steps. Ellie followed him. Upstairs she tiptoed into her room, careful not to waken Marie. She lay in her bed and listened. Across the room Marie sighed in her sleep.

From downstairs came the sound of angry voices raised, then lowered, raised, then lowered again, like the pulsating flame on a burner. Ellie strained to hear shreds of her parents' conversation.

"...were you *think*ing?" That was her father's voice, and it was punctuated by the sound of something being crashed down on a table, making china rattle.

"They're my new friends, okay?" replied Doris.

Ellie couldn't catch the next bits of the argument, but a few moments later she heard Doris say quite loudly, "I do, too, have friends!"

"Who? Who are your friends?"

"It doesn't matter. That's not the point anyway, is it? This is really about my success —"

"It's really about you staying out until all hours," Mr. Dingman interrupted Doris. "And about you doing whatever you damn well please. You always get your way, don't you? That's some example to set for the children."

His voice trailed away, into the kitchen, and Ellie could no longer make out the harsh words. She turned on her side and concentrated on the moonlight, on the way it fell in slanted shafts across Marie's bed. She lay very, very still until the arguing had stopped, and all she could hear was the muted sounds of her parents closing up the house for the night — her father letting Kiss out, then calling her back inside, locks being turned, windows being lowered. Eventually she heard soft footfalls on the stairs and the voices of her parents in their bedroom. Ten minutes later the house was absolutely silent. When Kiss appeared in her doorway, Ellie whispered her name and patted the end of her bed. Kiss would spend part of the night with her, part of the night across the room with Marie, then move to Albert's room, dividing her affection equally among the Dingman children.

Sparrows on a Wire

On the night before the first day of school in 1963. the night before Ellie's first day of sixth grade, Holly phoned Ellie three times and Ellie phoned Holly two times. Five discussions about what to wear the next day, and by morning, Ellie still did not have a clear idea for a safe outfit. The problem with dressing like a chameleon was that it could backfire. Sometimes boring called as much attention to itself as flashy or weird or wrong.

"How about our sleeveless dresses?" suggested Holly in their third conversation. "With saddle shoes."

"I don't think they're wearing saddle shoes anymore," said Ellie.

"Who aren't?"

"Maggie and Nancy and Donna."

Holly let out a prolonged sigh. "Wear that new dress Doris just bought you."

"No, it's pink."

"Well, I'm going to wear my sleeveless dress."

"Okay, I will, too."

But when Ellie stood in front of the bathroom mirror

the next morning, stood there naked except for her old summer dress, she knew it was all wrong. For one thing it was far too short. Ellie had grown two inches over the summer and now she stared at her skinny legs with their bony knees and almost nonexistent calves and wondered how long it would take for her body to look like Doris's. Doris's legs were firm and muscled and shapely, and her breasts (Doris called them her cleavage) were full and round and pressed tightly against whatever she was wearing on top. Her waist was narrow, her hips just wide enough so that they undulated when she walked. Ellie was skinny and straight from top to bottom, like a column. Furthermore, her lank hair was brown, her eyes were hazel, and after a summer outside on Witch Tree Lane, her skin had darkened to the color of a walnut, so that she was all one color. She was a skinny, monochromatic pole.

And the dress looked hideous on her. If she wanted camouflage, it was not the way to go.

Back in her room, Ellie tried on and discarded skirts and dresses until Marie called up the stairs, "Ellie! Doris says you're going to miss the bus and she's not driving you!"

"Okay!" Now Ellie was wearing a yellow dress that Doris had found on the reduced rack at Korvette's. It had ruffles around the bottom and lace at the neck. Doris hadn't been able to resist it because it was so cheap. Since it was the longest dress Ellie owned, she left it on, even though it was far from camouflage, and flew down the stairs to the kitchen.

Fifteen minutes later she was standing at the end of Witch Tree Lane with Albert, Marie, Holly, the Levins, and the Lauchaires. Kiss and Pumpkin, on opposite sides of the street, watched the kids from their front porches.

"Excuse me, I might throw up," said Domi.

"Don't," said David.

Domi didn't, but Ellie knew how she felt. Her own heart was pounding. Albert kept craning his neck down Route 27, in search of the bus. Holly twisted her hands. They were all waiting for the torture to begin.

The Witch Tree Lane stop was the last one on the route. By the time bus #5 rolled to the corner, everyone else on the route would have been picked up. And as many of them as possible would have crowded to the windows for their first glance at the knot of outcasts. They would want to see Selena Major's daughter, the girl who didn't know who her father was. They would want to see what weird, stained, grubby clothing the Frenchies were wearing. They would want to see those Jew kids, see if the boys had on their yarmulkes, the black hats that looked like tiny pot holders. And they would want to take a peek at Doris Day Dingman's children, since her run through Bosetti's was still fresh in their minds.

Ellie knew all this and took a tiny step back, a step away so she could see the Witch Tree Lane kids as the kids on the bus would see them. It was true that the Lauchaires were wearing clothes that appeared to have been plucked out of the hamper before they'd found their way into the washing machine. And that on the back of Domi's head was a big rat's nest of slept-on hair. And that both children wore sneakers without socks, their chubby legs smudged with dirt and grass stains from the previous evening's games of Tag and Statue.

And it was true that Selena's daughter and Doris's older daughter were wearing clothes that, Ellie now realized, looked more appropriate for church than school. (Holly had decided to dress up her outfit with ankle socks, black patent-leather flats, and a stack of her mother's bangle bracelets.)

But the rest of the kids looked all right. And David and Allan were not wearing their yarmulkes.

"Allan," Rachel said suddenly, "remember, no matter what the kids say, you do not have cooties."

"What?" said Allan. Today would be his first time riding the bus to Washington Irving. The year before, when he was in kindergarten, Mr. Levin had driven him to and from school. But now he was old enough for the bus.

"Cooties," Rachel repeated, and was about to launch into an explanation when Ellie put out her hand and shook her head at Rachel.

"But —" Rachel started to say.

"There it is," Albert said suddenly in a flat voice. "The bus."

The kids, except for Allan, grew rigid.

The bus was groaning along Route 27, and now it wheezed to a halt at the corner. Sure enough the windows on the Witch Tree Lane side were crowded with faces. Allan looked at them, looked at the arms hanging out — even though this was not allowed — at the noses pressed to the glass, then up at Ellie, back to the faces, back to Ellie, and finally said, "Are we famous?"

"Yes," Ellie replied.

The bus door scraped open, and Ellie could hear the sounds of the kids scrambling to reclaim their seats. She and Holly glanced at each other. Then Ellie took Allan's hand and helped him up the first high step.

"Where do we sit?" asked Allan, bewildered, as he and Ellie reached the aisle and stood before the rows of faces.

"In a seat, idiot," said a boy.

"But not in mine," said another.

"And not mine. I didn't have my cootie shot."

"I didn't have my Hebe shot."

Ellie surveyed the bus. The kids were spread out so that the Witch Tree Lane children couldn't stick together unless they sat in the very last rows.

Allan turned his face up to Ellie's. "I want to sit with you," he whispered.

Behind them, the rest of the Witch Tree Lane kids were standing uncertainly.

"Find seats, please," said the driver. "I don't have all day."

"Okay," whispered Ellie to Holly. They had thought this might happen, had discussed it with the rest of the kids the day before. They had a battle plan, and they were prepared.

Ellie sat down heavily in the nearest seat, pulling Allan into her lap.

"Cooties! Cooties!" cried the girl next to them. She edged away until she was smashed up against the side of the bus.

Behind Ellie, Holly sat down. Two rows back, Etienne sat next to a girl, one of his classmates. She slid away from him, holding her nose.

It was when Ellie heard someone tell Marie that the seat next to her was saved that Ellie stood up and said quietly, "This is the last stop, Lorraine. Either let Marie sit there, or go sit somewhere else." She raised her voice. "We are not sitting in the back anymore," she added, recalling the times when Marie and Rachel had gotten carsick.

"The dingbat speaks," said the boy across the aisle from Ellie.

"Are we ready back there?" asked the driver wearily.

Heaving great sighs, several of the kids stood up and rearranged themselves so that the Witch Tree Lane kids could sit together. The driver watched this in the rearview mirror, his arms folded across the steering wheel. At last he straightened up, put the bus in gear, and headed back to Spectacle.

School would be so much easier, Ellie thought, if she and the other Witch Tree Lane kids didn't have to take the bus. Waiting at their bus stop prevented them from being the slightest bit anonymous. Of course, most Spectaculars knew who Doris Day Dingman was, and what Selena Major had done. And it was hard to miss the Lauchaire kids in their unkempt clothing, or the fact that David, Rachel, and Allan were absent from school on the Jewish holidays. But not starting off each day as the kids at the Witch Tree Lane bus stop would have been a step in the right direction.

Washington Irving Elementary, one of two small elementary schools in Spectacle, was a long, low brick building five blocks from Bosetti's that housed thirteen classrooms, a gymnasium that was also the auditorium, a library, a music and art room, a cafeteria that Ellie hated and tried to avoid, a nurse's office, and the principal's office. Outside were two playgrounds — a smaller one for the younger children and a larger one for the older children.

When the bus drew up in front of the school, Ellie and the Witch Tree Lane kids remained in their seats until the other kids had rushed past them and scattered across the playgrounds.

"Holly and I are going to take Allan to his classroom," Ellie said to Marie. "Can you find yours by yourself?"

"I'm not a baby," she replied, kicking at gravel, and stomped away, leaving Domi and Rachel to run after her. Albert had already disappeared.

Because Allan at first didn't want to be left in his new classroom, Ellie and Holly reached their own classroom just as someone (was this their *teacher?*) was about to close the door. Ellie came to a dead halt at the sight of the person, and Holly ran into her from behind.

The person, whoever he was, looked almost exactly like Jimmie Dodd from *The Mickey Mouse Club.*

Ellie peered around him at the number on the classroom door. Twelve. That was their room number, all right. But this couldn't possibly be Mr. Pierce. Ellie had found out just recently that she and Holly were to have a new teacher instead of old Mrs. Fox who, over the summer, had decided to retire. And Ellie had spent many hours in the last few days wondering about Mr. Pierce. She had decided he was old, like Mrs. Fox, and had pictured him with a gray crew cut and round eyeglasses. Furthermore, she had decided he was strict and stern and unsmiling. And that he had a fascination with the Revolutionary War, and would ask his students to write many compositions about it.

And now here was Jimmie Dodd holding the door open for them, grinning, not knowing where they lived or who they were or anything about their mothers.

Maybe he was a teacher's aide.

"Girls?" he said. "Are you in this class?"

Ellie hesitated. "I guess so. Are you Mr. Pierce?"

"Yup. Come on in."

Ellie glanced over her shoulder at Holly and could tell just by Holly's raised eyebrows that she, too, thought Mr. Pierce looked like Jimmie Dodd. For the first time in her life, Eleanor Roosevelt Dingman stepped into a new classroom feeling pleased and hopeful.

Then she and Holly peered around Mr. Pierce, and Ellie's stomach dropped. Sitting in a line in the first row of desks, like sparrows on a telephone wire, were Maggie Paxton, Nancy Becker, and Donna Smith. And a new girl, whose name didn't even matter because Ellie could tell that she was just another Maggie. Or Nancy or Donna. Four of them, perched in their seats with perfectly combed hair; bright, tidy dresses; clean blue binders and spotless pencil cases on their desks; ankles crossed neatly under their chairs. Pert, confident faces were turned toward Mr. Pierce, with eyes that narrowed slightly (but not enough so that Mr. Pierce would notice) when they caught sight of Ellie and Holly.

Ellie turned to Holly in disbelief. Maggie, Nancy, and Donna. The most popular girls in their grade, and the most scornful of Ellie and Holly. They had been the most popular for several years running, and although there were two classes in each grade, these girls always seemed to wind up together in the same room, with Ellie. When Ellie had complained about this to Doris over the summer, Doris had said, "Look at the odds. They'll probably be split up in sixth grade, like you and Holly were last year." This made sense, and Ellie had been relieved.

And now here they were again, a cruel trio — joined by a look-alike fourth.

Still grinning, Mr. Pierce closed the door behind Ellie and Holly. Ellie searched the room for available desks, avoiding the four faces in the front row.

"Ladies," said Mr. Pierce, indicating a desk in the back row and another behind the new girl. He held his hand out as if he were a waiter showing Ellie and Holly to a table in a fancy restaurant, like when Lucy and Ricky went out to dinner once on *I Love Lucy*.

Ellie sidled between Nancy and Donna, eyes lowered, and made her way to the back of the classroom. She slid into her seat and, even though Jimmie Dodd was standing up there in front of the blackboard, she allowed herself to escape into her private place, to block out the sparrows in the front row, the concealed smirks. She fastened her eyes on the back of Holly's head and didn't say another word until recess.

Lunch came just before recess, and Ellie and Holly spent it as they always did, at the back of the cafeteria, eating apart from the other students, silently and quickly, before escaping to the library. In the library they usually read until it was time for their classmates, now scattered about the big kids' playground, to line up. Then they would hurry outside, join the end of the line, and return to their room.

On this first day of school, the girls huddled in a corner of the library as soon as they had bolted down bologna sandwiches and cartons of milk, but they didn't bother to choose books.

"He looks exactly like Jimmie Dodd!" cried Ellie softly.

"I know!" said Holly. "He could be his twin."

"Maybe he is his twin."

"Well . . ."

"So, what about the new girl?"

The new girl, whose name they now knew was Tammy White, had taken them by surprise. Had taken Donna and Maggie and Nancy by surprise, too.

"Did you see?" said Holly. "Nancy asked Tammy if she would sit with her at lunchtime and Tammy said *maybe.*"

Hardly anyone turned down an invitation from Nancy or Maggie or Donna, certainly not a new student.

"Really?" said Ellie.

"Yes. And did you see the way she was looking around the room?"

Ellie had seen that. Tammy had surveyed every kid in the class with her confident, appraising gaze, even the popular girls, who were used to being the appraisers, not the appraised.

"She's pretty, don't you think?" asked Ellie.

"Beautiful. Maggie and the others think so, too. They're scared."

"Maybe they've met their match," said Ellie, remembering something she had heard on television.

Holly giggled. "Oh, well," she said.

"And maybe Tammy will be different. Maybe she'll start a new group of popular girls."

"She did sit with Nancy and Maggie and Donna at lunch, though."

"I know. But *she* chose *them.* I saw," said Ellie. "*She* invited *them* to sit with *her.*"

Holly flipped the pages in a dusty atlas. "I heard Donna say she thinks Mr. Pierce is cute."

"He is cute!"

"I know, but I think she has a crush on him. I mean, a real crush, not like the kind we have on Jimmie Dodd."

"She can't have a real crush on Mr. Pierce. He's too old."

Holly shrugged.

Ellie peered up at the clock above the librarian's desk. "We have to go," she said.

Holly sighed and heaved herself to her feet. "All right." She paused. "You saw what happened on the way to the cafeteria, didn't you?"

Ellie sighed, too. "Yes." She had watched Maggie position herself in front of Holly, lock eyes with her, and jump from side to side, blocking her way as Holly tried to step around her. A wordless challenge.

"It's going to start again," said Holly.

"I know."

Ellie hoped Holly would say, "Oh, well," but Holly merely dusted off her dress as she stood up and said, "Come on. We don't want to be late."

Someone of Grand
Importance

Ellie kept her house key in her right sock. She figured that way it would be nearly impossible to lose. She didn't like to carry a purse, and had stopped wearing the key on a chain around her neck after the day in third grade when Maggie had reached over during a times tables lesson, yanked the key from the chain, and later flushed it down the toilet in the girls' room. Deep inside Ellie's right sock the key nestled under the arch of her foot, or sometimes under her toes. It was a little uncomfortable during gym class, but no one knew it was there, and it couldn't fall out. And Ellie needed it in order to let herself and Albert and Marie into their house after school. Unless Doris left home and forgot to lock the door, which happened pretty often.

At the end of their first day of school the Dingman children exploded out of the bus doors, followed by the rest of the Witch Tree Lane kids. The afternoon ride was somewhat less torturous than the morning one, since with each stop more and more kids disembarked until, for five blissful minutes, the Witch Tree Lane kids had the entire bus to themselves. During this time Holly would cross her legs prissily at the ankles and say to anyone who came near her, "No, no, please — do not dirty me with your cootie germs." And Albert and David would turn around in their seats and call out names to the empty bus behind them: "Stupid-head! Goat-breath! Turd!" But they were careful to leave out names such as Dirty Jew and Frenchie, which they never found funny.

By the time the bus came to a stop at Witch Tree Lane, the children were giddy, especially Allan, who had had no idea that a bus ride could mean standing on the seats and yelling out bad words in a gleefully rude manner.

"We'll see you in a minute!" Ellie called to the others as she and Albert and Marie hurtled across their yard. When she reached their front stoop she sat down hard on her bottom, tugged off her shoe, then her sock, and reached inside for the key.

"Hey!" said Albert from behind her. "The door isn't locked."

"Doris forgot again," said Marie.

"Oh, well," said Ellie.

"Where did she say she was going to be this afternoon?" asked Albert.

"I don't remember. Dance class?"

"Hey, wait," said Marie. "Her car's here."

Sure enough. There it was, right in the Dingmans' driveway.

"Doris! Doris!" called Marie as she ran inside.

"I'm upstairs!" Doris's voice floated through the stuffy, summer-hot rooms, and Ellie took note of the dirty breakfast dishes still sitting on the table, of Kiss's empty water bowl, of overflowing wastebaskets.

Marie charged upstairs with Albert at her heels. Ellie started to follow them, then stopped to fill the water bowl.

"Hi, Kiss," she said, stooping to pat her, and Kiss flopped over on her back, an invitation for a belly rub. "So what's Doris been doing all day?" Ellie asked her. "Come on. I'd better go upstairs and find out."

Albert and Marie were in their parents' room, lying side by side on the bed, eyes fixed on Doris. Ellie and Kiss joined them, Kiss stretching out full length along Albert's back, looking blissful.

"Doris!" Ellie exclaimed. She tried to take in the room, which was awash in discarded items of clothing. Slips, dresses, skirts, pants, stockings, garter belts, blouses, and even a bathing suit were tossed everywhere and trailed into the bathroom. "What are —"

"I," said Doris, before Ellie could finish her question, then she repeated *"I"* as if she were someone of grand importance, "have been invited to model in Harwell's very first Fall Fashion Show!"

"Invited?" repeated Albert. "I thought the fashion show was your —"

Ellie elbowed him in the side, and he rolled away from her, causing Kiss to slide onto Marie.

"You're really going to be a model?" asked Marie, her voice rising to a squeak. "Like the ones in magazines?"

"Yes. Exactly like those," said Doris.

"Can I be in the show, too?"

"No, Marie, this is just for women's clothing."

Albert glanced around at the garments littering the room. "Are you modeling your own clothes?" he asked.

"Oh, no, of course not. This is just for practice. I'll be modeling the latest fall fashions. You should see some of the things." Doris's face grew dreamy.

"Like what?" Marie asked, sitting up.

"Like, oh God, like some of those really incredible things you'd see on *The Jetsons*."

"*The Jetsons!?*" Ellie cried. "What? What are you talking about?" She was beginning to have a very bad feeling about the Fall Fashion Show.

"I mean, these clothes are true high fashion," said Doris. "Not just some collection of blouses or sweater sets. Harwell's plans to showcase the latest fashions from Paris and New York and . . . and . . . Albany."

The fashion capital, thought Ellie.

"You have never seen clothes like the ones Harwell's

wants to start selling. And I'm the cause of it all. If I hadn't had the idea for a fashion show, Mr. Harwell — he said this himself — would never have had the courage to try to import these lines of designer clothes."

"All the way from Albany," murmured Ellie.

"And so I have *got* to start practicing. Luckily I can do that with my own clothes."

"Practicing what?" asked Albert.

"Oh, quick changes, the proper way to show off a bathing suit, that sort of thing."

"What do bathing suits have to do with fall clothes?" Albert wanted to know.

"Cruise wear, darling. Use your head." Doris tapped her temple.

Ellie rested her chin in her hands and watched as Doris stripped off the blue dress she'd worn to Bosetti's, then handed a stopwatch to Albert. "Time me," she said. "I want to see how long it takes to get into a complete outfit. Don't start until I say go."

"Okay," said Albert, who loved to time things. He set the watch, then waited for Doris's command.

Doris gathered up a blouse, a yellow skirt and sweater set, stockings, flat shoes, and some jewelry. "I better be prepared to accessorize," she said. Then, turning to Albert, she added, "Go!"

While Albert stared at the watch, Ellie and Marie stared at Doris, who was a flurry of activity. When the entire outfit was on, she stood in front of the children, breathing heavily, and cried, "Okay, stop!"

"Three minutes and thirty-seven seconds," said Albert.

"Not bad," said Doris.

"How long do professional models take?" asked Ellie.

Doris shot her a glance, not sure if Ellie was serious.

"I'll bet they take the exact same amount of time," said Marie loyally.

"You're all out of breath, though," said Albert. "You'd better practice some more. You don't want to be puffing and panting when you're walking around Harwell's in the fancy clothes."

"Well," said Ellie, "when the show is on, someone will probably be helping you. Right, Doris? They'll have a dresser or whatever it's called handing you the clothes and stuff. That will speed things up."

Doris flashed Ellie a grateful look. "Yes, I believe they will."

"Doris," said Marie, "will you get to wear a crown like you did at Bosetti's?"

"No, hon." Doris leaned over the dresser and examined her eye makeup. "Crowns are for beauty queens, not models."

"I want you to be a beauty queen again."

"Well, I'd like to be one again, too. Although I don't know if tactfully I was one at Bosetti's."

Technically, Ellie thought automatically.

"But you won a contest. And Mr. Bosetti called you the Bosetti Beauty and gave you a crown," said Marie.

"I know. I'm just not sure if . . . well, it isn't like I rode in a parade or . . ." Doris trailed off. She pulled away from the mirror, straightened up, turned around, and faced her children. "You know," she said, "what this town needs is a good parade."

"We have one," said Albert. "The Memorial Day parade. It's good."

"Yes, but I was thinking of something a little more fun."

"Like what?" asked Ellie. Already she had a bad feeling. Another bad feeling. The look in Doris's eyes made Ellie's thoughts turn to chameleons and ways to distance herself from her mother.

"Like with tap dancing and other forms of entertainment."

"You don't tap dance," Ellie said suspiciously.

"Who said she's going to be in the parade?" asked Albert.

"No one did. But Eleanor is very smart," said Doris.

"She's got a good brain. All three of you do. You're living up to your names, and I'm proud of you."

"So you *are* going to be in the parade?" asked Marie.

"There's no parade yet!" said Albert.

"No, but there's going to be," said Doris. "A Harvest Parade. To celebrate Spectacle's harvest tradition."

"Our harvest tradition?" repeated Ellie.

"Bringing in the sheaves and all. It'll be great. Good for town morale. They should hold it near Thanksgiving. The stores can make floats to advertise their Christmas merchandise, and we can have pumpkins and apples —"

"Tap-dancing pumpkins and apples," whispered Albert to Ellie.

"You mean people dressed like pumpkins and apples marching in the parade?" asked Marie.

"Or floats with real pumpkins and apples on them. Whatever. And the highlight of the parade will be the last float. That will be the one for the Harvest Queen."

"And the Harvest Queen gets to wear the crown!" cried Marie.

"Exactly."

And, thought Ellie, somehow Doris will get to be the Harvest Queen.

Doris stood in the bedroom looking thoughtful, a

tube of mascara in one hand, a container of blue eye shadow in the other.

"Doris?" said Marie. "Can I tell you about school now? You said to wait until you were done practicing for the fashion show."

"Sure," said Doris. "Tell me all about it. I know second grade is going to be a real good year for you. I bet you'll be in the highest reading group again."

"Did you know they switched me out of Mrs. Geary's class? I thought I was going to be in her class and they moved me and three other kids into Miss Riddel's class. Did you know that was going to happen?"

"I might have gotten a letter about it," said Doris, peering into the mirror again.

"Well, they split up me and Domi. She's still in Mrs. Geary's class."

The phone rang then and Doris grabbed for it. "Hello?" She turned her back on the Dingman children. "Oh, *hi!*" she exclaimed. She glanced over her shoulder at Ellie and Albert and Marie, turned away, then turned back to them again. "Hold on a minute," she said into the receiver. "Kids," she whispered, "run along outside now, okay? I've got to take this call. Go and play outside for a while."

Ellie rolled over and slid off of her parents' high bed. "Come on," she said to Kiss, who jumped down after her.

"I don't want to go," said Marie.

"Well, we have to," Ellie replied. "Anyway, I told the other kids we'd see them in a few minutes, remember?" She ushered Kiss and her brother and sister into the hallway, and closed the door to the bedroom quietly behind her.

Don't Look Now

Ellie thought Mr. Pierce was amazingly cute (but she didn't have a crush on him, since he must have been at least twenty-five), and after observing him for a day or two, she decided he was an okay teacher. For one thing, he allowed her to remain in the back of the classroom. In fact, he didn't even assign seats. On the second day of school he told his students that they could sit wherever they wanted; that if they liked the seats they were in, they could stay in them. So Ellie had remained in the back, the four chirpy popular girls had remained in the front, and Holly, desperate to escape the scrutiny of the popular girls, had managed to switch with Anita Bryman and was now sitting in the back next to Ellie.

Mr. Pierce, Ellie realized on the third day of school, paid a lot of attention to the appearance of his classroom, but not much attention to the students themselves. As long as the room was tidy and the desks were neatly arranged and everybody was reasonably well behaved, Mr. Pierce was happy. And Ellie was relieved. She was out of reach of Maggie and the sparrows, who wouldn't want to disappoint Mr. Pierce by so much as turning around in their seats. Anything they might do to Ellie and Holly would have to be done very subtly or outside of the classroom, unlike the year before when Maggie and Nancy and Donna were emboldened by the fact that they didn't like their teacher and didn't care if she caught them misbehaving. So far they hadn't tried much. Every day, Ellie wore her plainest, dullest clothing, and she and Holly steered clear of the girls on the way into school and ran into their classroom at the last possible moment. They ate their lunches in the back of the cafeteria, then escaped to the library and, later on, the playground, joining the very end of the line of their classmates, knowing the sparrows would be at the head of the line. In class, Ellie looked only at Mr. Pierce, the blackboard, or her own work.

Two weeks passed without incident.

Then Doris came to school.

She interrupted a morning spelling quiz. Mr. Pierce was standing behind his desk reading out words and sentences. "*Restaurant.* We are going to eat dinner in a *restaurant* tonight. *Restaurant.*" Before him, twenty-two heads were bowed over sheets of composition paper neatly numbered from one to twenty in two columns.

Mr. Pierce paused. Then he said, "*Enough.* I hope there will be *enough* food at the restaurant. *Enough.*" He grinned, as if he had made a joke.

Tammy and Nancy and Maggie and Donna were laughing politely when the door to the classroom was flung open and in walked Doris.

Ellie dropped her pencil and turned to Holly in horror.

Doris's hair had been swept up to new heights. It towered above her head, adorned with glittery combs in the shape of butterflies. Perched on her nose was a pair of enormous sunglasses, the ones that slanted into the shape of cat's eyes, and made the world nearly black, causing Ellie to wonder how Doris had navigated the dim school hallways. Worst of all, Doris was wearing a red shift so tight that even from the last row, Ellie could see the lines of her girdle through it. Also, she was wearing her high high heels, and lots of plastic jewelry, loud and sparkly to match the butterflies in her hair.

Doris snapped her gum and waved to the kids, her wave taking in the entire room, as if she were a politician putting her audience at ease. But she didn't see Ellie in the back, so after a glance over her shoulder at the number on the door, she said, "Are you Mr. Pierce?"

"I am. And you are . . ."

"Doris Day Dingman." Doris inclined her head ever so slightly toward Mr. Pierce. "Eleanor's mother," she said in a husky voice.

"Eleanor . . ."

"Eleanor Dingman?"

"She means Ellie," spoke up Maggie, jerking her thumb over her shoulder in Ellie's direction.

Doris scanned the back of the room, spotted Ellie, and said, "Oh, *hi*, darling!"

"Hi." Ellie gave Doris a small wave.

Doris's gaze returned to Mr. Pierce, and she crossed the room to him, her hips swaying lightly. Ellie now saw that Doris was clutching a paper bag. She held it out to Mr. Pierce. "My Eleanor forgot her lunch," she said.

Ellie heard a muffled snort of laughter from somewhere nearby. She glanced around the room. Several students were covering their mouths or, heads bowed, were searching through their desks, shoulders shaking. In the front row, Maggie, Nancy, and Donna gaped at one another, Mr. Pierce momentarily forgotten. But Tammy was looking at Doris with an expression of awe, lips slightly parted, hands gripping the edge of her desk. She watched Doris, then turned around to look at Ellie, eyes wide.

Mr. Pierce took the bag from Doris, smiling at her, and Ellie was gripped by the need to see the fourth finger on Mr. Pierce's left hand. No ring.

Doris faced the class again briefly, then turned back to Mr. Pierce. "Well," she said in the husky voice that made Ellie think of wine and candles and darkened rooms, "'bye."

"Good-bye . . . Mrs. Dingman," replied Mr. Pierce.

Ellie, her face hot as a flush spread across her cheeks, stared down at her hands and did not look up when Doris called to her, "See you this afternoon, sweetie," as she glided through the door and out into the hall.

Eleanor Roosevelt Dingman, one of the best spellers in all of Washington Irving Elementary, missed the next two words on Mr. Pierce's quiz because she couldn't hear his voice. She thought she might faint, and only managed not to because she didn't want to attract further attention to herself.

Bzzzzzzz went a wood-handled steel saw in her ears. Black dots massed in front of her eyes, and her arm slipped across her desk. Then Holly's hand was resting on Ellie's wrist. "Are you okay?" she whispered.

Ellie nodded. The buzzing faded, and her eyes cleared.

"Number eleven," Mr. Pierce was saying.

Ellie glanced at her paper and saw the last word she had written, *enough*, printed neatly beside the numeral 8. What had happened to nine and ten?

"Unexpected," said Mr. Pierce. "We had an *unexpected* visit from Mrs. Dingman. *Unexpected.*"

Ellie dutifully wrote *unexpected* as light laughter drifted to the last row of desks. A few minutes later, when she had written the final word of the quiz and passed her paper forward, she allowed herself to escape to her private place.

That day, Ellie and Holly had an argument in the cafeteria.

"I just want to buy milk," said Holly. "That's all."

"But you'll have to stand on line," said Ellie, who was flattened against the back wall. "Come on, skip it."

"You don't have milk, either."

"I don't *need* milk!"

"I'm thirsty. And I have a bologna sandwich and potato chips. They're going to make me even thirstier."

"Get a drink from the water fountain."

"I don't want water with bologna and potato chips. I want milk."

"Then I'm going to eat right now and go to the library without you," said Ellie. She looked around the cafeteria, knowing that today of all days she and Holly should stay out of sight.

"Fine," said Holly. "Eat by yourself then."

"Fine. I will."

Holly marched off and Ellie had just decided that maybe she shouldn't eat at all, should find a trash can, pitch her troublesome lunch, and get to the library as soon as possible, when someone tapped her on the shoulder.

"Ellie?"

Ellie whirled around. Tammy was standing behind her, her lunch tray balanced on the palm of one hand. She was alone, thank God. The other sparrows were not in sight.

"Yeah?"

"I just — I just want to say," Tammy began, and Ellie hugged herself, arms folded tightly across her chest, "I just want to say that . . . Did I see your mother's picture in the paper a few weeks ago?"

"What?" Ellie was caught off-guard; she had been waiting for an insult, or even a quick jab in the ribs, so fast that no teacher would notice.

"I mean, well, we had just moved here," Tammy continued. "It was at the end of the summer. And my mom bought the paper the first time we went to the grocery store. And there was a picture of this really pretty lady wearing a crown. And now I . . . Was that your mother?"

Ellie nodded. "She won a contest."

"She was the Bosetti Beauty!" exclaimed Tammy. "That *was* your mother. Wow. She is really something. I never thought she was anybody's mother."

When Ellie didn't reply, only peered to the front of the cafeteria, searching for Holly, regretting their argument, Tammy said, "So is she a model or something?"

"What?"

"Your mother. Is she a model? Or an actress? She doesn't look like anybody else in Spectacle."

"Well," said Ellie, loosening her grip on the lunch bag, "she sort of is, I guess. She's been in some plays. And soon she's going to —"

"On *Broadway*?" squeaked Tammy.

"What?" said Ellie again.

"Plays on Broadway? In New York City?"

"Oh, no. Not like that. Plays here. In Spectacle. With the community theater group. And she's going to be a model at Harwell's."

"You're kidding. I didn't know there were models at Harwell's."

"Doris is going to be the first."

"Wow," said Tammy. "You call your mother Doris?"

"She insists on it." Ellie glanced over Tammy's shoulder and now caught sight of Maggie, Donna, and Nancy sitting in a row before untouched lunch trays, their eyes fastened on Ellie and Tammy.

"How does she get all those jobs?" Tammy wanted to know.

Ellie squirmed. "She has a résumé. And sometimes she goes to auditions. And she takes classes."

"Does she sing and dance?"

"Sort of."

"Because I want to be a model one day, but I can't really sing or dance, so I was wondering if you have to know how to do those things."

"Not for the modeling, I guess —"

"How does she find out about auditions?"

"She just watches the newspaper —"

"Gosh, she's beautiful. Doris. Does she make everyone call her Doris? I wish my mother looked like her."

"I —" Ellie searched the lunch line and saw that Holly was standing in front of the cashier, paying for her carton of milk. She was about to tell Tammy that she had to meet Holly, when Tammy took a step back from Ellie and looked her up and down.

"You're not a thing like Doris," she said, and shrugged. "But you sure are lucky she's your mother." She waved to the others. "I'd better go. See you."

"See you," Ellie said, and watched Tammy slide onto the bench across the table from Donna. "Holly!" Ellie called then. "Holly!"

"What," said Holly in a flat voice. "I thought you were mad at me."

"*Tammy* just talked to me!"

"What?"

Ellie, tugging Holly toward the doors of the cafeteria and talking in a loud whisper, told her about the conversation with Tammy. "What do you think it means?"

Holly paused and turned around. "Don't look now, but they're all staring at us. Tammy and Donna and Nancy and Maggie."

Ellie immediately turned around.

"I said, 'Don't look now'!"

"I couldn't help it. I wanted to see."

"I don't think this is good," said Holly.

"It must be a joke. Right?" said Ellie.

"Definitely. Hurry."

Ellie and Holly escaped from the cafeteria.

Sunday

From time to time on Witch Tree Lane something scary would happen at night, something scary and often not noticed until the light of day. Marie called these things simply the Bad Things. And this term was reserved only for the nighttime incidents. Sometimes she would say that something was bad (riding on the bus was bad, not being in Domi's class was bad, Albert's bursts of temper were bad). But a Bad Thing was all the mailboxes on the street being sprayed with a can of pink paint. Or finding the word QUEER scrawled on Miss Woods and Miss Nelson's driveway. Or a rock being thrown through the front window of the Levins' house.

Nobody on Witch Tree Lane ever saw anyone doing the Bad Things. And the police didn't take much interest in them. But the people on Witch Tree Lane had to live with them, and they were scary.

On a Sunday afternoon at the end of September another Bad Thing was discovered. It made Ellie's knees weak, and destroyed what had been a perfectly nice day, one that had started with the Witch Tree Lane kids roaming their street in a pack. They had met up shortly after lunch. As Doris had pulled out of the Dingmans' driveway in the Buick on her way to something (Ellie had forgotten what), David, Rachel, Allan, Domi, Etienne, and Holly had swarmed out of the Levins' yard, David calling, "Hey! Hey, Ellie! What are you guys doing?"

"Nothing," said Ellie.

"Is anyone home at your house?" (David meant any parents.)

"No." Mr. Dingman was on the other side of Spectacle, finishing up an addition on a house.

"What's in your refrigerator?" asked Etienne.

"Nothing."

"Popsicles in the freezer," said Albert.

The nine children crowded into the Dingmans' kitchen, finished off one box of ice pops, and started another. Then they went to the Lauchaires', who had a refrigerator in their garage, and helped themselves to sodas.

"Now let's jump on our trampoline!" said Allan.

"After Popsicles and soda?" asked Ellie. "No way."

"What should we do then?" asked Rachel.

"Hey, there's Miss Nelson," said Holly.

Ellie looked across the Lauchaires' yard to the house at the end of the street. She could see a figure in a loose brown dress covered by a roomy apron with big kangaroo pockets on the front. The figure was kneeling in the garden, her toes sunk into the earth behind her so that her sandals flopped off of her heels. "Come on!" said Ellie.

And the Witch Tree Lane kids ran through the yards to Miss Nelson.

"Good lord in heaven!" exclaimed Miss Nelson as she heard them approach.

"Do we sound to you like a herd of elephants?" asked Domi.

"At least," replied Miss Nelson.

"What are you doing?" Rachel wanted to know.

"She's *gardening*," said Albert.

Rachel stuck her tongue out at him, then said, "If you know so much, tell me *exactly* what she's doing."

When Albert shrugged, Miss Nelson said, "I'm getting the flower beds ready for winter. Would you like to know what's in the garden now?"

Rachel nodded, and Ellie could hear Miss Nelson say, "These golden flowers are chrysanthemums. . . ." Her eyes drifted from Rachel and Miss Nelson to the Witch Tree, where Allan was peering at the knothole. He had grown enough lately so that he now had to lean over slightly in order to look at it.

Allan must have been thinking the same thing, because he exclaimed, "Ellie, do you see? I don't have to stand on tiptoe anymore!" He traced the profile of the witch with his forefinger. "Tell me again about the tree," he said.

"Well, it's really just an old oak," Ellie replied. "People call it the Witch Tree because of the face —"

"And because of its evil powers," said David in a low voice.

"Oh, it does not have evil powers," said Ellie. "Don't pay any attention to him, Allan."

Miss Nelson stood slowly, clutching her knees. She straightened up, put her hands against her back, stretched, then brushed dirt from her apron. "I wish people understood," she said

"Understood what?" asked Holly.

"The Witch Tree." Miss Nelson walked stiffly across the yard and rested one hand affectionately on the gnarled bark.

"You mean," said Albert, "how that witch face materializes into a real live witch at night that floats out of the tree and over our street —"

"Noo!" howled Marie.

"I was thinking," said Miss Nelson, "of what this tree has seen. It's been standing here for more than two hundred years. It was here before the Civil War, it was here before cars and TVs and radios. It was here before there was a Witch Tree Lane or any of our houses, and even before Spectacle became a town. When it first stood here it was part of a forest."

"Is it a boy or a girl?" asked Domi.

"It's a *tree*," said Etienne.

"It's been here since before I was born," said Allan.

"Since before a lot of people were born," agreed Miss Nelson.

"Since before Marie Curie and Albert Einstein and Eleanor Roosevelt were born," said Marie solemnly.

"It's seen more than I'll ever see," said Miss Nelson.

"Do you think it has eyes?" Marie asked, touching the knothole. "Do you think it really sees things? Maybe it sees who does the Bad Things at night."

"I think it keeps watch over us," said Miss Nelson. Then she added, "A shame. A beautiful old tree like this, watching over us, and people say it's evil. It's just a shame."

The front door to the ladies' house opened then, and Miss Woods stepped onto the porch. "Hi!" she called to the children, waving a batch of letters in the air.

Ellie watched her tromp down the porch steps and make her way along the cracked tar of the driveway to the mailbox. She tugged at the door of the box, then tugged harder. "What on earth —" said Miss Woods, puffing as she pulled again. She stuck the letters in her mouth, planted her feet firmly on the street in front of the mailbox, and tugged at the door with both hands. The box remained shut.

"What's the matter, dear?" called Miss Nelson.

"Damn box won't open." Miss Woods gave another terrific yank and Ellie saw the post pitch forward. But the door wouldn't budge.

"Well, don't . . . don't strain yourself." Miss Nelson left the children and hurried to the end of the driveway. "Be careful."

Miss Woods paid no attention. She flung the letters to the ground and, after one final pull, leaned forward to examine the box. "It's — it's been — someone glued the damn thing shut."

"Dear, please stop swearing." Miss Nelson inclined her head toward Ellie and the others, who were still standing by the Witch Tree, fascinated by this turn of events.

"I'll swear all I want." She paused, her breath coming in large raspy gasps. "I'm going to call the police."

"Is it a Bad Thing?" asked Marie, standing on tiptoe to whisper in Ellie's ear.

"Maybe," replied Ellie. "I mean, it must be. The box was okay yesterday."

Miss Nelson stooped to gather the letters. Then she put her arm around Miss Woods. "Come on inside now."

Ellie watched the ladies as they walked arm in arm back to their porch. Then she found herself turning to look down the street. Her eyes took in the other houses, one by one — the Lauchaires', the Levins', Holly's, her own. She scanned windows, walls, mailboxes. Nothing looked broken or defiled or out of place. And she knew that her own mailbox was in working order.

The children drifted away from the tree, Marie and Rachel and Domi deciding to play indoors, the boys heading for the Levins' trampoline.

Holly eyed the mailbox. "Maybe we can get it open," she said.

But they couldn't.

After pulling so hard they were afraid they might uproot the post, they wound up in Holly's bedroom.

"Where's your mom?" asked Ellie, lying on Holly's pristine bedspread. Everything about Holly's room was pristine, from the ruffled curtains at the windows to the neat rows of books and stuffed animals and china horses on the shelves. Holly's mother had seen a picture of a girl's bedroom in a magazine when Holly was six, and had copied it for her daughter. She insisted that Holly's room remain in immaculate condition. Nobody could say that Selena Major didn't keep a perfect house.

"Probably over at Mick's," Holly replied. She stroked

Pumpkin, who lay curled in her lap, one paw covering his eyes as if the light in the room were more than he could bear.

"The new guy?"

Holly nodded, her mouth full of Bazooka.

"Do you like him?"

"Nope." She blew an enormous bubble that collapsed on her nose.

"How come?"

"Because," she said, pulling at shreds of pink gum and trying not to disturb Pumpkin, "because ... it's hard to describe. He's not mean, exactly. But I don't think he has any respect for Mom. And I kind of think he takes advantage of her. Like, he makes fun of her for cleaning houses. She'll come home in her dirty clothes, her hair up in that cloth, and he'll say, 'Hard day at the office, dear?' And then he'll ask to borrow money from her."

"Well, what does he do that makes *him* so great?" asked Ellie. She had stretched out on Holly's bed, but now she propped herself up on her elbows, frowning.

"That's just the thing. He's not even working right now, which is why he needs to borrow money. He lost his job. But when he had one he was the manager of a diner in Pious."

"Huh," said Ellie.

"I avoid him as much as I can."

"Does your mother really like him?"

Holly nodded. "I think so. She spends enough time with him."

"Don't you wish," said Ellie, "that our mothers were friends?"

"They like each other," replied Holly, surprised.

"Oh, I know. But, I mean don't you wish they were really *friends?* Like Laura Petrie and Millie Helper on *The Dick Van Dyke Show.* You know, calling each other on the phone all the time, and going over to each other's houses for coffee, and talking about their problems and asking for advice."

"Like we do," said Holly, "except we don't have coffee."

"Doris needs someone to talk to. Does your mother have anyone to talk to?"

"Her girlfriends from high school. They talk all the time."

"They should talk your mom out of Mick."

"Believe me, they try to," said Holly.

Ellie flopped down on the bed again and pretended not to see that Holly was eyeing her Mystery Date game. Ellie hated Mystery Date, hated thinking about boys, about dating boys; couldn't imagine a boy touching her, or being interested in her skinny, one-color body. "What do you think about the Bad Thing?" she asked, examining her ragged fingernails.

"It's the first one in two months."

"But it's the third one that's happened to Miss Woods and Miss Nelson. The third in a row."

Holly sighed. "I know. Which reminds me. That's another reason I don't like Mick. Mom told him about someone writing 'queer' on the ladies' driveway, and he laughed."

"Huh," said Ellie again. "She should dump him."

It was because of *The Ed Sullivan Show* that Ellie forgot about the Bad Thing. The show came on on Sunday evenings and it put Doris in such a good mood that she would make supper. The menu on the night of the day the Bad Thing was discovered was canned hash, canned okra (from the Bosetti's shopping spree), and canned peaches in heavy syrup. Dessert was a cake from Deising's that Doris had gotten for half price because HAPPY BIRTHDAY POLLY! had been scrawled on the top but no one had picked up the cake. "We even have hors d'oeuvres," said Doris, pulling out the jar of Snappies from Bosetti's. "Okay, get your TV trays, everyone. The show is about to start."

The five Dingmans hurried into the living room with their plates of food and settled themselves behind the TV trays. Kiss lay at Ellie's feet.

"Doris, can I —" Marie started to say.

But Doris hushed her. "It's starting! It's starting!" she said.

And there was Ed Sullivan, standing on the stage of his theater in New York City, looking somehow both proud and uncomfortable.

"Ha!" cried Doris when the first commercials came on. "I could be on the show. I know I could do something. I could dress up my hand like Señor Wences. Or I could do a dramatic reading. One day I'm going to audition for Ed Sullivan."

"When Annette Funicello auditioned for Mr. Walt Disney she sang 'Ac-cent-tchu-ate the Positive,'" spoke up Ellie.

"Well, I'm not going to sing," replied Doris. "That's not my strong suit."

"What is your strong suit?" asked Albert.

Mr. Dingman looked up from his plate of food, waiting for Doris's answer.

"Drama," replied Doris. "And I *swear* — one day I am going to audition for the show."

Ellie's father lowered his eyes again, and Ellie thought

she saw him shake his head ever so slightly, but she couldn't be sure.

"Oh, Doris, you say that every week," said Marie.

Which was true. But this time Ellie heard something different in Doris's voice. Different enough so that Ellie caught her breath and glanced over her tray and across the room at Doris's face to see what had changed in it.

Harwell's Fall Fashion Show

Harwell's Fall Fashion Show was heavily advertised in Spectacle's two newspapers. The ads didn't mention Doris, though, which disappointed her. "I don't understand," she said. "This is their first fashion show. It's a big deal. Where's my name? I should think they'd want to use it. After all, I'm going to be the Harvest Queen in the parade." Plans for the parade were in full swing, and Doris was to ride on the last float as a beauty queen, just as she had hoped.

"I think Harwell's wants to publicize their clothes, not the model," said Ellie. "It's the clothes they want to sell."

"Well, I'm the one who's going to sell them," said Doris.

"I thought you were going to model them," said Marie.

"Same thing," said Doris. "And they better pay me well, too."

"Didn't you work out the pay ahead of time?" asked Albert.

"Sort of."

Doris was sitting cross-legged on the living room

floor, two newspapers spread out around her. "Wow! 'The Town Topics' has a huge ad for the fashion show! Look at this. One whole entire page!" she exclaimed.

Ellie peered over Doris's shoulder. "I'll bet a lot of people will see you," she said.

"I bet more would come if they knew who they were going to see."

"Oh, well," said Holly, who was sitting behind Ellie, braiding her hair. "People will still see you. When does the show start?"

Doris jabbed at the ad, and Holly let go of Ellie's hair long enough to read, "'Come help us kick off Harwell's first Fall Fashion Show on Friday night!'"

"That's tomorrow night," interjected Albert.

"Opening night," added Doris.

"'Free refreshments! We will be open until nine o'clock!'" Holly continued. "Wow, Doris. Are you nervous?"

"Nope," said Doris. "I was born for this."

The Dingmans didn't get to see Doris's opening night at Harwell's. Mr. Dingman was working late on an indoor job, trying to cram in all the projects he could before the cold weather arrived. So Ellie stayed home with Albert and Marie, made popcorn for them, and told them they could read in their beds until Doris returned.

Doris swooped through the front door shortly after ten o'clock, wrapped in the glory of her evening.

"Hello?" she called.

"Doris!" Marie flew downstairs, still carrying her copy of *The Bobbsey Twins and the Mystery at Snow Lodge*. Albert was right behind her.

"How was it?" asked Ellie, who had been reading in the living room, one eye on her book, one eye trained out the window at the dark street with its shadows and secrets.

"Wonderful," replied Doris breathily. "Where's your father?"

"Right here." The door had opened again, and Mr. Dingman stepped through it.

"Oh, darling, there you are. I wish you had been at Harwell's tonight," said Doris. "I was a star."

Mr. Dingman leaned down and kissed her cheek. "I'm sure you were."

"Will you come see me tomorrow?"

"Tomorrow? Sure. We finished the job tonight. You were a hit, huh?"

"Mr. Harwell said it went better than he could have imagined. You should have seen all the people. They clapped and cheered. And the outfits I got to wear! Oh, they were something. Mr. Harwell said he wants the show to run the entire week, all day every day. Except Sunday."

"Then we'll come tomorrow," said Mr. Dingman.

"You mean Ellie and Albert and me, too?" said Marie, glancing hopefully from her father to her mother.

"Sure," said Mr. Dingman.

"Can the other kids come?"

"What, all of them?" asked Mr. Dingman.

Doris beamed. "Why not?"

"Yippee! I'm a cowboy!" hooted Etienne.

"Me, too!" shouted Albert. "I'm riding the range!"

"You kids settle down back there!" called Mr. Dingman from the front of his truck.

All nine of the Witch Tree Lane kids were crowded into Mr. Dingman's pickup. The youngest ones — Allan, Domi, and Marie — were squeezed into the cab next to Mr. Dingman. The others were gleefully riding in the back. "In the open air," Etienne said. They weren't allowed to do this often, but the Fall Fashion Show was a special occasion.

"I'm not leaving until every one of you is sitting down," Mr. Dingman went on, leaning out of his window now, and peering back over his shoulder.

The six kids in the back abruptly flopped down on the dusty metal floor, and Mr. Dingman pulled slowly out of the driveway and turned onto Route 27.

"Wah-hoo!" yelped David, but he remained seated.

Ellie eyed the boys, then turned to Holly and whispered, "Why'd we have to come in the truck like this? We look like hillbillies."

"Oh, well," said Holly.

In downtown Spectacle, Mr. Dingman parked several blocks from Harwell's, to Ellie's relief. As the Witch Tree Lane kids piled out of the truck, Mr. Dingman gave them their town instructions. "Okay, older kids are in charge of younger kids, and Allan, Domi, and Marie, each of you has to hold somebody's hand. Somebody who's older than you," he added as he saw Domi reach for Marie.

Ellie hung back as they walked along King Street. She was finding it very hard to blend in, what with the Lauchaires and their odd assortment of clothing, and her harried father surrounded by eight children and topped off with Marie, who was now riding on his shoulders and "giving his hair a stir," as she said.

"Come on, Ellie," said Holly. "Hurry up. We're almost there."

"Then why do I have to hurry up?" Ellie said, and hated herself for being crabby.

Holly shrugged. "I don't care." She ran ahead.

Ellie straggled into Harwell's several steps behind Holly and her father and the kids. She saw the frown on the face of the woman at the information desk as she watched Mr. Dingman, with his stirred-up hair, set Marie on the floor. Saw the frown deepen as the woman caught sight of Etienne Lauchaire in shorts and a woolen stocking cap, then expanded her view to include the rest of the children, most of them scruffy. And saw that she forced the frown off her face as Mr. Dingman approached her, but wasn't able to replace it with a smile.

"Excuse me," said Mr. Dingman, smoothing down his hair.

"Yes?"

Ellie, still guilty over snapping at Holly, whispered, "She has a face like an old potato."

Holly grinned.

"Can you tell me where Doris Dingman is modeling the fashion clothes?"

"Modeling the . . . ?" the woman's voice trailed off.

"She's our mother," spoke up Marie. "We're the Dingmans."

"Well, not all of us," said Albert. "Six —"

"Just go look in the store," the woman interrupted him. "She's walking around. You'll see her somewhere."

Ellie stepped in front of her father and said sweetly to the woman, "You've been a *wonderful* help. Thank you *so* much."

"Oh, you're wel —"

But Ellie turned away from her before she finished speaking.

"Ellie," said Mr. Dingman, a warning in his voice.

"Let's just find Doris," she replied.

"Look, there's a whole bunch of people over there," said Rachel. She pointed to a crowd on the other side of the store, in front of the Evening Wear Boutique.

"I see her! I see her!" cried Marie. "Wait. She's coming over here."

Ellie gripped Holly's hand and pulled her away, pulled her behind a display of neckties, then stood, her lips parted, as Doris swiveled toward them, stepping along an aisle that had been cleared of people.

"She has her own modeling runway," Holly whispered.

Ellie couldn't answer her. She was having a hard time believing that the woman swishing by was her mother. She didn't look glamorous, exactly. Not like Grace Kelly. But she was stunning in her own way, her long, tanned legs peeking through the slits of the evening gown, a glittering necklace (probably not real diamonds, but still) positioned in just such a way as to make a person very aware of Doris's voluminous chest. And she had put on so much black eyeliner that she reminded Ellie of an Egyptian queen.

For a moment Ellie was rooted to her spot behind the neckties. Then she heard Marie call, "Doris! Hi, Doris!" and the spell was broken.

Ellie stepped forward, smiling, but Doris continued down the aisle, a faraway expression on her face.

"What's she looking at?" asked Ellie. She had thought Doris would be sweeping the crowd with her gaze, as she had done in Ellie's classroom. But while Doris's shoulders and hips turned this way and that as she went slinking through the store, her head remained oddly stiff, her expression bland.

"Oh, she's doing what all the famous models do," said Holly.

"What do you mean?"

"They all look like that. It's *sultry*."

Ellie turned her attention to the clingy evening gown Doris was wearing. It was black, dripping with sequins, and puddling down around her feet so that Ellie expected her to trip over the bottom of it.

"I'll bet no one here has ever seen anything like that," said Holly.

Ellie, taking in the crowd in Harwell's, was pretty sure Holly was right. She noticed two salesgirls, dressed in suits with nylons and low-heeled shoes, glance at each other, then at Doris, then at each other again before erupting into giggles and rolling their eyes. Across the runway Ellie saw two young men fasten their eyes on Doris. The eyes slid down her body, up, down again, and then the men grinned in a way that made Ellie think of the boys in the cars riding along Route 27, honking at Doris in her bathing suit. And made the two saleswomen smirk and shake their heads.

She looked around for her father and saw that his own eyes were fastened not on Doris, but on the men. And she looked away quickly, down at the ground, at a button someone had lost.

"Ellie! Hey, Ellie!"

A familiar voice was calling, and Ellie turned around.

"Hi!" Tammy White had stepped between Ellie and Holly. "Ellie," she said, "this is so *cool!* Wow!"

"Hi, Tammy," said Holly.

Tammy turned briefly to Holly. "Hi," she said, then faced Ellie again. "Gosh, look at that dress. Does Doris get to keep the clothes?"

"Keep them? I don't know. I didn't think about that."

"Either way, she's so lucky. *You're* so lucky."

"Tammy, Tammy." Someone thrust out an arm and grabbed Tammy's hand.

"Oh! Oh, hi, Maggie," Tammy said and, with a glance at Ellie, slid back into the crowd.

"'Bye," Ellie called after her.

"What a jerk," muttered Holly.

Ellie felt a tug at her sleeve. "Ellie? Doris didn't say hi. She didn't even look at us," said Marie.

Ellie stooped down. "She's busy. She has to be professional."

"Well . . . that was rude."

"Did you like her dress?"

"I guess."

Doris had disappeared, had floated somewhere out of sight.

"Can we go now?" asked Marie.

"Already? I'll bet Doris will come out in another dress if we wait a few minutes."

"I don't need to see another dress."

"How about ice cream?" said Mr. Dingman.

Marie brightened. "Really? We can get ice cream?"

"Sure. Ice cream for everybody. Let's go to the Dairy Queen."

Mr. Dingman and the Witch Tree Lane kids pushed through the crowds. As they approached the information desk, Ellie called, "Thanks again for all your help," to the potato-faced woman, then followed Albert outside into the autumn air.

"Look, there's Doris modeling in the window," said David.

"Why's she holding so still?" asked Allan.

"I think she's pretending to be a mannequin," Holly replied.

"I don't care. Let's go get the *ice* cream," said Marie.

"Okay, okay, keep your shirt on," said Albert.

"Daddy, pick me up, please." Marie leaned imploringly against Mr. Dingman, and he reached down to her.

There was a line at the Dairy Queen, and they had to wait nearly ten minutes before the boy behind the counter, paper cap perched crookedly on his crew cut, said sullenly, "Can I help you?"

"He should say, '*May* I help you,'" Domi whispered to Ellie.

"Ten medium vanilla cones, please," said Mr. Dingman.

"Ten?" repeated the boy.

"Ten." Mr. Dingman indicated the kids.

"Okay-ay," said the boy in a bored, singsong voice.

"I hope we're not putting him to too much trouble," Ellie said to Holly.

The Witch Tree Lane kids sat at two picnic tables next to the Dairy Queen and waited. Mr. Dingman carried their cones to them two by two, starting with the younger children. Ellie was just taking the first lick of her ice cream when she looked across the table at Allan and saw that he was slurping the last of his out of the bottom of the cone, which he had bitten off.

"Allan!" she exclaimed. "Did you finish already?"

"I was hungry." He patted his stomach.

Mr. Dingman sat down next to Ellie and ate his own cone while Ellie stared out at King Street, remembering Tammy, remembering the lady with the potato face, remembering Doris glide by Marie in Harwell's.

"Well, how about one more peek at Doris before we go home?" asked Mr. Dingman a few minutes later.

"No," said Marie.

"We have to walk by Harwell's, anyway, to get to the truck," Albert pointed out.

"All right, but you can't make me look."

"Whatever."

They had just reached the group of people gathered outside Harwell's window when Allan said quietly, "I don't feel well," then leaned over and threw up on the sidewalk.

"Oh, *ew!*" someone squawked, jumping backward.

"Hey, he rides my bus," a boy said, pointing to Allan.

"He's the Hebe," his friend replied.

"Hush," said a woman, paling at the sight of the vomit. "That isn't polite." She pulled the boys away.

"Dad," said Ellie, peering into the Harwell's window and realizing that Doris, lost in some world of her own, had no idea that Allan was sick or even that her family had returned and was part of the crowd. "Do something."

Mr. Dingman patted Allan on the back, and he leaned over and threw up again.

"Here, Allan." Ellie pulled a napkin from the Dairy Queen out of her pocket and wiped his mouth with it. "You just ate too fast, that's all. Come on. Let's go home."

Ellie and her father and the Witch Tree Lane kids hurried down King Street, Mr. Dingman carrying Allan. Behind them, Doris twirled and turned and posed in the window of Harwell's.

Circus Girl

"Ellie?" Tammy White stepped in front of Ellie and Holly as they zipped into their classroom one Friday morning, hoping to scurry to the back unnoticed.

Ellie stumbled, and Holly grabbed for her arm, steadying her.

"Oh, I'm *sorry*," cried Tammy. "Sorry, Ellie. I didn't mean to scare you. . . . So, how are you?"

It had been a week since the end of the Fall Fashion Show; nearly two weeks since Tammy had spoken to Ellie in Harwell's, had spoken to her at all.

"I'm fine."

Next to Ellie, Holly shifted from foot to foot. "Hi, Tammy," she said.

"Hi, um . . ."

"Holly," said Holly.

"Oh. Yeah."

"How's your — how's Doris?" asked Tammy.

Ellie peered around Tammy, needing a view of the front row. Donna, Maggie, and Nancy sat primly at their desks, eyes on Tammy and Ellie, their expressions unreadable, at least to Ellie.

"She's fine, too."

"Does she have any more modeling jobs coming up?"

"I don't think so."

Holly shifted position again, then leaned back against the bulletin board, knocking two paper oak leaves to the floor.

"Oh," said Tammy, with the briefest of glances at Holly. "You can go."

"What?"

"You can *go*." Tammy inclined her head toward the back of the room.

"It's okay, Holly," Ellie murmured, and Holly walked backward to her desk, not taking her eyes off of Ellie.

"So what were you saying?" Tammy cocked her head at Ellie.

"That Doris isn't going to be doing any more modeling. That I know of. But she's going to be the Harvest Queen in the parade."

Tammy clutched at Ellie's hands. "Parade? What parade?"

"The Chamber of Commerce decided to hold a Harvest Parade this year. On the weekend before Thanksgiving. Doris is going to ride on the last float as the Harvest Queen."

"Wow. Is that like a beauty queen or something?"

"I guess."

"Man, that is so cool."

The door to Room 12 opened then, and Mr. Pierce entered just as the bell rang.

"I'd better go," said Ellie.

"Wait. Sit at our lunch table today, okay?" Tammy glanced at the sparrows behind her.

"Well —" said Ellie.

"Ladies?" said Mr. Pierce, raising his eyebrows at Ellie and Tammy.

"See you at lunch!" Tammy called as she slid into her seat.

Ellie ran to the back of the room.

"What was all that?" Holly whispered.

But Mr. Pierce was peering at Ellie over his reading glasses.

"I'll tell you later," Ellie whispered back.

That morning Ellie bit all of her fingernails down as far as she could without making anything bleed. She wished Tammy had been more specific when issuing her invitation. Did she and the other girls actually want Ellie to join them for lunch, or had they merely asked her to sit at their table? It was a big table. Ellie could sit at it and still be several seats away from Tammy. A person had to be very, very careful when dealing with girls like Tammy.

Furthermore, had the invitation been extended to Ellie alone, or could Holly go, too? Ellie didn't want to bring along an uninvited guest, but she couldn't imagine deserting Holly. She also couldn't imagine what might happen if she turned down an invitation from the sparrows. A person didn't do that. A person didn't want to risk making the sparrows mad.

Ten minutes until the bell would ring signaling lunchtime for the sixth graders, and there was not a thing left to nibble at on Ellie's fingers. One pinkie actually was bleeding now, and her heart was racing. She had spent math period composing a note to Holly explaining her dilemma, but then had been too nervous to pass it to her.

She kept her eyes on the clock. Eight minutes until lunch. Five minutes until lunch. Four —

The door to Ellie's classroom burst open, and Doris swept through it, followed by Albert and Marie, who were looking dazed.

"Darling!" Doris cried, and Ellie realized she was addressing Mr. Pierce.

Ellie heard a giggle and kept her eyes trained on her brother and sister, standing hesitantly by the classroom door.

Mr. Pierce, who had been grading papers at his desk, stood up quickly, wiping his hands on his pants. "Mrs. Dingman. What a pleasant surprise," he said, extending a hand. Then he added, "What brings you here?"

"Circumstances," Doris began, "force me to take my children away immediately on important family business."

"Oh. I see. There's nothing wrong, is there?" asked Mr. Pierce.

"No, no, no. Not at all. And Eleanor will be back in school on Monday. I promise."

Mr. Pierce looked toward the back of the room. "All right, Ell — Eleanor. Gather up your things. Take your reading book with you and read chapter eleven over the weekend, please."

Ellie nodded. As she rummaged in her desk, she whispered to Holly, "I'm sorry. I'm sorry you have to ride the bus without me this afternoon. Sit with Allan, okay? I'll call you later." She grabbed her notebook and reading book, then reached back in her desk, grabbed the undelivered note to Holly, crumpled it up, and stuffed it in her pocket. "'Bye," she said, and slid out of her seat.

Ellie allowed herself a quick glance at the front row. Tammy was gazing adoringly at Doris. When she caught sight of Ellie, she gave her a wave and mouthed, "See you on Monday."

"Ta-ta!" Doris called as she pushed Ellie, Albert, and Marie through the door ahead of her.

"Ta-ta!" Ellie heard Tammy reply.

The Buick sped through the streets of Spectacle toward Witch Tree Lane.

"Doris, what's going on?" Ellie asked.

"Darlings, the most wonderful opportunity has come up," she replied as she careened around a corner.

"Slow down!" yelped Albert.

"You know Circus?" asked Doris.

"The circus?" said Marie.

"No. *Circus.* Those restaurants on the highway? The ones with the elephants on the signs?"

"And the big clowns out in front?" asked Ellie.

"Yes!" said Doris, temporarily removing both of her hands from the steering wheel.

"They have good hot dogs," said Marie. "Mrs. Lauchaire took Domi and me to one once."

"Well," said Doris, "Circus is looking for a Circus Girl. You know, to make TV commercials for them, and to pose for new signs and things. And since Circus is a local chain, the auditions are going to be held in several New York towns. One of them, Magnolia, is just two hours from here. And Magnolia is right near where I grew up."

"Near Baton?" asked Ellie.

"Near Nan and Poppy?" asked Marie.

"Yes," said Doris. "And the audition is tomorrow. So we're going to stay at Nan and Poppy's. We'll drive there this afternoon."

"Dad, too?" asked Albert, at the same time that Ellie said, "Why are *we* going?"

"Because your father just got a job with a crew way over by Charleston, and he won't be home until next week. So off we go!" said Doris gaily.

"We're really going to stay at Nan and Poppy's?" asked Ellie. She knew that for some reason Doris didn't get along with her parents and preferred not to see them. In fact, Ellie had met Doris's parents only once, when she was five, and remembered a skinny man and woman who hugged her a lot and told her she was beautiful. Albert had been three then and Marie just a baby, and they didn't remember their grandparents at all.

"Yup," said Doris. "We're really going to stay with them. It'll be the most convenient for everybody."

You mean for you, Ellie thought.

"Hurry now," Doris said as she wheeled the Buick into the Dingmans' driveway and jerked it to a stop. "Get your things packed. I want to leave as soon as possible."

"What should I pack?" asked Marie. And then she added, "Do I have a suitcase?"

"Oh, just use a paper bag," said Doris. "Eleanor, help her. I've got to call your father, and then go get my things ready. I better bring all my makeup and, let's see, probably three changes of clothes . . ."

"Ellie, can you help me, too?" asked Albert.

"Sure," Ellie replied, and headed for the kitchen, where she found a pile of grocery bags.

The Dingmans were back in the Buick in less than an hour. Doris was at the wheel, a pink traveling kerchief covering her hair. On the seat next to her were her bags, her makeup kit, the box containing her hair rollers, and another box containing her hair dryer, the plastic hose emerging from it like an exhaust pipe.

In a row in the backseat sat the Dingman children and Kiss. At their feet were four paper bags. Ellie had packed them — one for her, for Albert, for Marie, and a small one containing Kiss's kibble, her blanket, her leash, and two toys. Doris had forgotten about Kiss until she saw Albert coaxing her into the car.

"What's Kiss doing?" asked Doris.

"Coming *with* us," replied Albert. "We can't *leave* her here."

"Oh, no. Of course not."

They sped down Route 27, away from Spectacle. Doris turned the radio on full blast and sang along loudly, just slightly off-key. The Dingman children sat silently in the backseat. Ellie gazed out the window. She watched the hills and woods give way to fields and isolated homes and tiny farming communities. Kiss's eyes began to close, and she fell asleep in Ellie's lap, her nose resting on her wrist. On either side of Ellie, her brother and sister grew drowsy, too, and Ellie felt them slide into her, their heads heavy against her shoulders.

The tractors and silos and stubby-looking fields began to rise and fall giddily as Ellie drifted into a dream. They disappeared and were replaced by a beach where she and Holly lay reading on a blanket while Tammy, Maggie, and Mr. Pierce played Marco Polo in the water.

"Marco!" shouted Tammy.

"Polo!" the others replied.

"Marco!" shouted Tammy.

"Here we are!" called Doris.

Ellie struggled awake. Two faces, an old man's and an old woman's, were peering through the car windows at the Dingmans.

"What on earth?" said the woman.

"Ta-da!" cried Doris. "I'm going to be the new Circus Girl!"

Nan and Poppy

Ellie shook the sleep from her head as Albert and Marie straightened up groggily, and Kiss awoke, startled, and erupted in frantic barking.

"Kiss! Shhh!" said Albert.

"Darlene, is that really you?" asked the man outside the car.

"It's really me," replied Doris.

The woman had jumped back as Kiss lunged at the window, but the man circled around to the driver's side, opened Doris's door, and leaned in to kiss her. "Well now, well now," he said.

The man was tall and thin, and so was the woman, and they reminded Ellie of the people in a painting she had once seen. An old man and an old woman standing stiffly next to each other, tidily dressed, the man holding a pitchfork. They were old and solemn, even stern, and dressed in simple clothes. Ellie had assumed they were husband and wife, although who knew? Maybe they were brother and sister, or old friends. But something about them said husband and wife — two people who had faced a difficult life together. Just the way something about Nan and Poppy said husband and wife, even if you didn't know them.

The difference between the couple in the painting and Nan and Poppy was that Nan and Poppy were lively and smiling and bustling. And scruffy. When Poppy stuck his head in the car, Ellie could see that he was wearing only a sleeveless T-shirt and dusty old dungarees, and that his sparse hair was sticking out in all directions from his head. And Nan's hair, even at this hour of the afternoon, was tightly wound around curlers, which were partially hidden by a hairnet. She was dressed in a housecoat, and on her feet, which Ellie had seen when Nan had jumped away from Kiss, were striped terrycloth scuffies. Her veiny legs were bare, no socks or stockings.

"Well, I never," said Nan, tentatively approaching the car again, now that Kiss had stopped barking.

"Doris! Didn't you tell them we were coming?" exclaimed Ellie.

"Oh, darling, I didn't have time. Anyway, they don't mind."

"Mind a visit from our own grandbabies?" said Nan. "Of course we don't mind. Come on out here and let me take a look at you," she went on as Ellie, Albert, and Marie fumbled for their paper bags. "Now, I'm your Nan, and this here is your Poppy. You probably don't remember us, but you did meet us once, when you were little bitties."

"I remember you," said Ellie shyly. She reached across Marie to open the door. "Go on out," she whispered. "Go hug her. Leave your bag here. I'll hold on to Kiss."

Marie slid slowly out of the car and stood uncertainly by the door. Ellie stuck her foot out and nudged the back of Marie's leg. Marie looked desperately over her shoulder at Ellie, then reached out and gave her grandmother the briefest of hugs.

"Oh, now, that's not a hug," said Nan. "This is." She enfolded Marie in her arms and squeezed her so tightly that Ellie heard Marie emit a small squeak.

Nan stuck her head in the car then and extended her hand toward Kiss, who sniffed it, then gave it a lick. "Ah. He's my friend now," said Nan. "The rest of you come on out of there and let me look at you, too."

Ellie let go of Kiss, who hopped out of the car and began sniffing the patchy lawn by the driveway. Then she climbed stiffly out of the car, pulling Albert after her. The Dingman children stood in a row, facing their grandparents.

"Well," said Nan. "Eleanor, Albert, and Marie. I'd know you anywhere. Look how beautiful you are, just look."

Ellie actually did look. She looked at Albert and

Marie, their eyes puffy from their nap, their hair snarled where it had been smushed against Ellie's shoulders. There were large holes in the knees of Albert's blue jeans, and something white and crusty just below the collar of Marie's shirt. Then Ellie looked down at herself. She wasn't quite as monochromatic now that her summer tan was fading, but she was as skinny as ever, with droopy kneesocks and scuffed penny loafers, the penny missing from the left one.

For a moment, Ellie took in the tableau her family made: two grandparents smiling fondly at three sleepy kids, Doris hovering in the background, uncertain and impatient. And then Ellie's stomach growled so loudly that Kiss looked at her in alarm, and Nan exclaimed, "My word! Whose stomach is talking? Come on inside and I'll fix you something to eat. Let's see, what time is it, anyway? Why, it's after three. What did you all have for lunch?"

"Nothing," spoke up Albert.

"And we passed two Circuses before I fell asleep," said Marie.

"Oops," said Doris. "I guess I forgot about lunch." She turned to her parents. "I always try to keep my figure slim and trim. Nobody wants a fat star," she said gaily.

"Don't mean the children need to be on diets, though," said Poppy.

Doris pulled the last of her things out of the front seat of the car and slammed the door shut with extra force. "Well, let's go inside," she said. "I bet you kids would like to see my old bedroom."

"Could we see it after we eat?" asked Albert. "I'm starving."

"Albert," said Doris, a warning in her voice.

"No, no, that's all right. We already offered," said Nan. "We'll have sandwiches now, and a big dinner later. You better get to the store for some extras, Father. Maybe a roast, and we'll need potatoes and another vegetable, and I better check my baking supplies."

"Righto," said Poppy. "Anybody need help with their bags?"

"I could use a hand," said Doris, who was standing amid her boxes and suitcases, clutching the hair dryer. "Eleanor, grab your things from the backseat."

Ellie retrieved the grocery bags from the floor of the car.

"Where are your suitcases?" Poppy asked her.

Ellie shrugged. "We didn't need much," she said. "This is just for a couple of nights."

"Well, now, who likes ham and cheese sandwiches?" Nan asked as she turned toward the house.

"Me!" cried Albert and Marie.

Ellie, her arms full of bags, whistled for Kiss, and followed the others through the front door.

From the outside, Nan and Poppy's little house was plain — dusty white with black shutters; a small front stoop, concrete crumbling; ragged rhododendron bushes under the front windows. But there was nothing plain about the inside.

"Ooh," said Marie as she glanced around. From where they stood, crowded into the entryway, they could see nearly the entire downstairs of the house — to their right, a living room (a sign over the fireplace read BLESS THIS MESS), to their left, a sort of den (a small embroidered pillow hanging from the doorknob read FATHER), and ahead of them the kitchen.

Ellie thought it was the most cluttered, most cheerful home she had ever seen. An upright piano was smothered by crocheted doilies, music books piled on and under the bench. The couch was stacked with pillows that Ellie thought Nan might have made herself. The walls were covered with pictures and photos. In the FATHER room was an old desk awash in papers, and a shelf with books and copies of *National Geographic* spilling off of it. In the kitchen was an enormous table, a bench on each side, and in the corner was a table with a sewing machine on it.

"Just put your things down anywhere," said Poppy.

"And come on into the kitchen," added Nan.

"I think I'll head upstairs," said Doris. "I have to decide what to wear tomorrow."

"Suit yourself," said Poppy.

Ellie set the bags on the floor by the front door. "Can I help you?" she asked Nan and Poppy as she followed them into the kitchen. "By the way, you can call me Ellie. And Kiss is a she. Is she allowed in the house?"

"Anyone's allowed in this house," replied Nan. "Never need to ask. Just go ahead and make yourselves at home. Father, why don't you show Albert and Marie the photo albums? Ellie, you help me."

Nan insisted on making two sandwiches per person, even though Ellie assured her that she and Marie would eat only one each, and that Doris wouldn't have any at all.

"Well, it never hurts to have extras," Nan replied. "Somebody might need a midnight snack. Now everybody come on in here and eat so's I have time to make us a good dinner."

Ellie wondered what they were going to do for the rest of the afternoon, how the hours would be spent, what everyone would talk about. With Doris holed up in her old room, the Dingman children faced their grandparents on their own. But there wasn't a single awkward moment. There wasn't even a moment of quiet.

Nan talked nonstop during lunch. As soon as the dishes had been cleared away, she said, "Now, do any of you know how to play the piano?"

"I can play 'Chopsticks,'" Marie said, and jumped up to demonstrate.

"Isn't that wonderful," Poppy said when Marie had finished, and Nan clapped her hands.

"I can play it fast, too," said Marie, encouraged, and played it both twice as fast and twice as loud.

"Bravo!" called Nan.

"Say, are you a fisherman?" asked Poppy, turning to Albert, who was sitting quietly at the table. Albert looked, Ellie thought, not exactly sullen, but as though he hadn't yet made up his mind about Nan and Poppy.

"No. I've never been fishing." Albert raised his eyes hopefully. "Are *you* a fisherman?"

"Well now, well now, I'll say I am," Poppy replied. "I go fly-fishing, mostly. If you come out in the backyard with me, I'll show you how to cast a rod."

"Father," said Nan. "The store?"

"Oh. The store. Well, how about if Albert and I go to the store first, and when we come back I'll show him how to cast a rod?"

"That's fine," said Nan. "Now, you girls, I guess you know how to make Barbie clothes, don't you?"

Ellie and Marie looked at each other. "Not really," said Ellie.

"We can't sew," added Marie.

"My land," said Nan. "Go on over there to that pile of scraps by the sewing machine." She paused. "You do have Barbie dolls, don't you?"

"Oh, yes. Two each," Marie assured her.

"Good. Pick out some scraps and we'll get to work as soon as I do a few things to start our dinner."

By the time dinner was ready that night, Ellie and Marie had sewn skirts for their Barbies and baked a cake with Nan. Albert had practiced casting a fishing rod and had tossed a baseball back and forth with Poppy, even though it had been nearly dark outside.

"Ellie," Marie whispered as they climbed the stairs to the tiny spare room under the eaves, "this is the best vacation I've ever been on."

"Me, too," agreed Albert. "Poppy is going to take me fishing for real tomorrow." He looked at the room they were standing in. "Is this the attic?" he asked.

"I guess," said Ellie. "I mean, I guess it used to be. Doris's room and Nan and Poppy's are downstairs."

"Did you get to see Doris's room yet?" Albert set his grocery bag on a cot.

Ellie shook her head. "She's been closed in there all afternoon. We'll knock on her door when we go downstairs for dinner. Here, Marie, you and I will share the other bed."

Marie stood on her tiptoes and peered out a small window, but darkness had fallen. She turned around again. "I like this room," she announced. "I like the whole house. I like Nan and Poppy."

Ellie smiled at her. "So do I. Come on, you guys. Nan said dinner was just about ready. Let's go find Doris."

They left their things on the beds and ran back down the stairs.

"Doris?" called Ellie.

There was no answer. But Albert said, "Hey, this must be her room. There's the hair dryer."

Ellie peeked inside. "Wow," she said. "It still looks like a kid lives in it."

"Look at all the trophies," said Albert. "What are they for?"

"I want to see them up close," said Marie. "Do you think we can go inside?"

"Sure," replied Ellie. "She said she thought we'd like to see her room, remember?"

Marie tiptoed through the doorway and peered up at

a shelf. "'Miss Teen Sunshine, nineteen forty-eight,'" she read, pointing to the writing on a gold cup. "'Miss Baton, nineteen forty-seven.' Ellie! Albert! Doris won beauty pageants or something! She has a million trophies!"

"Huh," said Ellie, who thought the room looked very much like Holly's, except for the trophies. On the white-painted bed were Doris's old dolls and stuffed animals, and on the shelves were china figurines and a set of Nancy Drew books and a pink jewelry box with a twirling ballerina inside. "Isn't it weird to think Doris was named Darlene when she lived in this room?" she added.

"Nan and Poppy still call her Darlene," noted Albert.

"Ellie! Albert! Marie!" Nan's voice floated up from downstairs. "Dinner!"

"Coming!" Ellie cried, and hurried her brother and sister from the room.

Dinner was served in the kitchen. Ellie plopped down next to Poppy and looked at the table. It was crowded with dishes — a roast and potatoes and green beans and salad and black olives and a basket of bread and a plate with a stick of butter on it.

"This is like Thanksgiving!" exclaimed Marie.

And Albert said simply, "Wow," as he surveyed the table.

Doris glanced up sharply, then turned on a smile. "For heaven's sake, anyone would think you kids had never seen food before. What they mean," she said to her parents, "is that it's so nice of you to put on this spread for us."

"Well, this is just such a wonderful surprise," said Nan. "Our only daughter and our only grandchildren, right here —"

"Does Susie Clinton still work at Gino's? I think I'll go look her up tonight," Doris said.

"You mean you're not going to visit with us?" replied Poppy.

"Nan is going to make fudge and popcorn," spoke up Marie.

"Well, how often do I get back to Baton, after all?" said Doris. "I have to see my old friends. They'll just kill me if they find out I was here and didn't even say hi."

"Well now, well now," said Poppy. He cleared his throat, lowered his head, and got busy buttering a potato.

After a little silence, Ellie said, "I haven't seen the photo albums yet, Poppy. Can we look at them after dinner?"

Poppy offered her a wavery smile.

That night, Ellie, Albert, and Marie fell asleep in the room under the eaves. It was nearly eleven o'clock when they said good night to Nan and Poppy and climbed the stairs. Doris had not returned.

"We'll see her in the morning," said Ellie.

"Whatever," replied Albert.

Good-Luck Charm

The next morning Ellie was awakened by dim light struggling through the narrow window over Albert's bed and by the smell of toast and bacon and eggs and coffee. She rolled over lazily and looked at Marie asleep on her side, her back pressed against Ellie. Once, when Ellie had spent the night at Holly's, she had awoken in a panic, unable to figure out where she was. There was a wall to her left that didn't belong there, and a floaty canopy over her head, and the window was in the wrong spot. But when Ellie awoke at Nan and Poppy's she was certain of where she was, certain she belonged there.

She glanced across the room at Albert, one arm slung over Kiss, who was stretched out next to him, and stood up to see out the window, but couldn't without disturbing her brother. So she pulled her jacket on over her nightgown and for a moment sat on the edge of her bed, breathing in the smells of breakfast. Then she tiptoed downstairs to the kitchen.

Nan was stirring something in a pot on the stove, and Poppy was setting the table.

"Well now, well now," said Poppy, smiling at Ellie. And Nan wrapped her in a tight hug.

Moments later, Albert, Marie, and Kiss thundered down the stairs and into the kitchen. "Good morning!" cried Marie as she plopped onto one of the benches.

"Morning," replied Nan cheerfully, planting a kiss on her head.

"Did Doris come home last night?" asked Albert. He stood in the doorway, looking defiant.

"Yes, she did," said Poppy. "Now come have some breakfast."

The Dingman children and Kiss ate breakfast with their grandparents. Outside, a chilly rain was falling. It dripped down the windows and rushed through the gutters. Fog rolled in, so thick that Ellie couldn't even see the house next door.

"I guess this means we can't go fishing," said Albert glumly.

"Not while it's raining this hard," Poppy replied. "Wouldn't be much fun sitting out in the boat in this weather. But don't mean we can't stay home and do something else just as much fun. What do you know about magic, Albert?"

"Magic?"

"Rodney the Great came to our school once," said Marie. "He did all kinds of tricks. He poured milk in his hat and then turned the hat over and the milk was gone. And he pulled a bunch of flowers out of his sleeve, and he made an egg disappear under a handkerchief."

"Would you like to learn how to do some magic tricks?" asked Poppy.

"You can do magic?" said Albert.

"Just a little," Poppy said modestly.

"Oh, he's got a whole big box full of tricks in the den," said Nan. "It'll take him hours to show them to you. He puts on magic shows all the time. Where was the last one, Father?"

"Over at the nursing home."

"Can you show me how to do the tricks?" asked Albert.

"Can I learn magic, too?" asked Marie.

"Sure thing," said Poppy.

"Or you can help me bake a pie," said Nan.

Ellie sat in her chair, sipping orange juice and thinking about the day ahead. She couldn't remember the last time she had been so excited about a rainy day. Magic tricks, pies, Barbie clothes, that row of Nancy Drew books in Doris's room.

"Yoo-hoo! Yoo-hoo, everybody!"

Ellie, her mind wrapped around the events of the day, turned slowly to see Doris descend the stairs into the living room.

"How do I look?" she asked. "Do I look like a Circus Girl?"

"You look beautiful," said Marie.

"What's a Circus Girl supposed to look like?" asked Albert.

"I'm not sure," replied Doris, who, Ellie thought, was dressed in a slightly tamer outfit than usual. For her audition, she had chosen a tight-fitting green and white dress and green pumps. Perched on her hair, which Doris had teased into a poof that cascaded down the back of her head like a waterfall, was a small green Jackie Kennedy pillbox hat. "I guess I should look like a spokeswoman. I figure I'll be standing around pointing things out and explaining them."

"You mean like Amana refrigerators?" asked Marie.

"Well, no," said Doris. "Like Circus Burgers. Or those clowns by the front doors. Or maybe where all the Circuses are on a big map of New York." Doris posed next to the oven, moving one hand across it as if she were pointing out cities and towns.

"And Eleanor," Doris continued, "I want you to come with me today."

"To Magnolia?" squeaked Ellie. "To the audition?"

Doris nodded.

"But we were going to bake a pie, and Poppy's going to show us his magic tricks —"

"I need you for formal support," interrupted Doris. "Really. I don't think I can do this without you. You're my good-luck charm."

"Aren't I a good-luck charm?" asked Marie, dropping her chin into her hand.

"Oh, sure you are, hon," replied Doris. "Eleanor is just older, that's all."

Marie scowled and Ellie said, "Doris, you've been on dozens of auditions without me. What do you need me for?"

"This is an important one. This isn't for the wicked fairy in some little play at the community theater."

"Or for the Spam Spread Girl," spoke up Albert.

Doris shot him a look, but said, "Eleanor, this is the big time. This is television. This could be my *break*. Don't you understand? You want me to get this, don't you? Just think what it could mean."

"Why, it could mean *The Ed Sullivan Show*," said Albert, smirking.

Doris put one hand on her hip. "Albert, go to your room."

"My room is in Spectacle."

"Albert."

Albert jumped up from the bench, cracked his knee on the table, and stomped out of the kitchen and up the stairs.

"Darlene, honey —" Nan started to say.

"Mother, I think I know how to handle my own kids. Eleanor, please be ready by ten-thirty. I want to make sure we get to Magnolia early."

"Okay, Eleanor, we're looking for number fourteen now," said Doris. She steered the Buick slowly along the main street of Magnolia, peering through the windshield as the wipers lashed back and forth. "It'll be on your side of the street. It's called the Town Theater, or something."

Ellie wiped fog from her window and tried to read the numbers over doorways. Finally she said, "There it is, Doris. Right there. The Little Town Theater."

"All right. Now if I can just find a parking space."

Ellie closed her eyes while Doris wrestled the car into a teeny space halfway down the block from the theater.

"Ready, hon?" said Doris as she turned off the ignition. "Let's make a run for it." Doris tied a plastic rain bonnet on her head and reached for the enormous black umbrella Nan had handed her as they left the house.

"Ready," replied Ellie, who was shivering in her jacket. She hadn't thought to pack a raincoat the day before.

Ellie and Doris sloshed along the sidewalk to the theater and hurried inside.

"Are you here for the audition?" asked a man sitting behind a card table that had been set up just inside the door. He was slouched in a plastic chair, toying with a pencil. He didn't glance up from the clipboard he was holding.

"Oh!" said Doris. "Yes! I don't usually look like this." She untied the rain bonnet, collapsed the umbrella, and handed both to Ellie. Then she patted her hair, feeling for the hat. "My! That is some weather. What a day for the audition. Are there many peo —"

"Name," said the man.

"Mine?" said Doris.

"Unless the little girl is auditioning."

"Oh. Um, Doris Day Dingman."

"Doris . . . Day . . . ," he repeated. "Can you spell Dingman for me?"

Doris spelled it.

The man jerked his thumb over his shoulder. "Go inside. You're number sixteen," he said, handing Doris a card with a large 16 printed on it. "Next," he added as the door behind Ellie opened and two more women stepped inside, shaking out their umbrellas.

It was after twelve-thirty when the auditions began. Forty-two young women were lined up on the stage in the theater, each holding her number card. Ellie had stayed with Doris until a man ("The *producer*," Doris had whispered) called the women to attention.

"Okay, go sit in the theater, Eleanor. You can watch from there," said Doris. "Wish me luck!"

"Good luck," said Ellie. "I'll keep my fingers crossed."

And so Ellie, still clutching the umbrella and Doris's rain bonnet, had moved to a row near the back of the theater, a row she had all to herself. Only a handful of people were sitting in the theater, all in the first few rows, holding papers and looking important.

"All right, ladies!" said the producer, standing up suddenly. "As you know, we need to find a Circus Girl. She will be the spokeswoman in our TV ads, she'll pose for print ads, and she'll do any other publicity that might arise. We need someone who is poised, gracious, and well spoken, someone who can represent Circus, someone who says Circus is a cheerful, fun, friendly, and *delicious* place.

"When I call your number, please walk across the stage from one side to the other, return to the center, face the audience, state your name, and then read what's written on the cue card."

The producer sat down again.

From the back of the theater, Ellie watched one woman after another walk across the stage. Several times the producer jumped up and called out, "Thank you!" before the woman even had a chance to say her name. He thanked one woman before she finished walking across the stage, and she left the theater in tears. Others, though, were asked to pose or to read cue cards, on which were written things like, "Circus, where your burger is served with a smile." Or, "Circus, now in six new locations!"

By the time the producer called, "Number thirteen!" Ellie's palms were growing sweaty. By number fifteen, her heart was pounding.

"SIXTEEN!" roared the producer, and Ellie jumped. Then she leaned forward, gripping the arms of her seat.

Doris stepped calmly from the wings, every hair in place. She walked slowly across the stage, smiling out at the audience the entire time. When she reached the other side she turned casually, still smiling, and walked confidently back to center stage, "my name," she said in a voice as smooth and rich as chocolate ice cream, "is Doris Day Dingman." She continued to smile at the producer.

The producer smiled back at her. Then he nodded toward the woman holding the cue cards.

Doris glanced at the first card and read, "'Here at Circus, burgers are served with a smile.'" Cheerfully, she pantomimed setting a plate on a table.

The producer indicated that Doris should read the next card. And the next and the next. Doris read them flawlessly, her smile never wavering.

Ellie relaxed in her chair.

Much later, when the last woman had taken her turn, the producer stood up once again. "Ladies!" he called. "Everyone onstage, please. Form a line."

Twenty-eight women were left and they lined up along the front of the stage.

"Very nice work," said the producer. "I'm going to call out some numbers now. If you hear yours, take one step forward. Ready? Three, seven, sixteen, eighteen, twenty-five."

Doris and four other women stepped forward.

"Thank you," said the producer. "You ladies in back may leave. You five in front, please stay behind."

Ellie's mouth dropped open. She expected Doris to jump up and down and clap her hands, but Doris stood, smiling and casual, and waited for the producer to speak again. Doris did offer Ellie a small, private wave, though, and Ellie grinned at her.

"Ladies," said the producer, "my assistant is going to give each of you a scene to rehearse. Please return tomorrow morning at eleven and be prepared to read it. I'll make my decision then. Have a good evening."

Not until Ellie and Doris had left the Little Town Theater and were walking back to the Buick did Doris grab Ellie's hand and say in a loud whisper, "I got a callback! I got a callback!"

Leaving Baton

"I got a callback!" Doris announced the moment she opened the front door to Nan and Poppy's house.

"Watch this!" called Albert, rushing at her with a purple scarf in one hand and a small silver ball in the other.

"I can do magic!" cried Marie, holding an egg aloft.

"What? What's this?" asked Nan. She emerged from the kitchen, wiping her hands on a dish towel.

"I got a callback," Doris repeated. "There were forty-one other girls there for the audition, and the producer only asked five of us to return tomorrow. I have a scene to rehearse and everything."

"Well now, well now," said Poppy. "This *is* exciting."

"You have to go back tomorrow?" repeated Marie. "You mean we get to spend another night here? Nan, Poppy, we get to spend another night here! Doris, do you want to see a magic show? Me and Albert learned so many tricks. We're going to put on a show for you. When do you want to see it?"

"Oh, later, hon," said Doris. "I've got to rehearse. I

don't have much time to prepare." She started up the stairs.

"But —" said Albert. He dropped his hands to his sides, and the scarf trailed to the floor.

"Aren't you going to put on a show for *me?*" asked Ellie. "I want to see a show. Unless Nan needs me to help her with something."

"No, no. You sit down right there, honey," said Nan.

Ellie plopped onto the couch. "I'm ready," she said.

Albert stuffed the scarf in his pocket. "It would be better if Doris was here, too."

That evening, after Ellie and Albert and Marie had telephoned their father, after dinner, after Doris had said she had rehearsed enough and had gone off with her friends again, and after Albert and Marie had climbed the stairs to the spare room, Ellie sat at the kitchen table with her grandmother.

"Nan? Did Doris *always* want to be a star?"

Nan poured out two cups of tea from a pot with ATLANTIC CITY scrawled on it in very fancy writing, and pushed one toward Ellie.

"Well, she always liked being the center of attention, that's for sure. She never was shy. Any chance to perform . . . there was your mother."

"We saw the trophies in her room. Are they all for beauty pageants?"

"Mostly. But she won a talent contest when she was in junior high. Won by reciting that poem by Edgar Allan Poe. The one about the talking bird. 'Quoth the raven, "Nevermore."' I never did understand what that was about. I'm not sure your mother did, either. But she sure said it beautifully."

"How old was Doris when she met Dad?"

"Oh, goodness. Now let me see. Eighteen, I guess. And they'd up, run off, and married in the space of four months. He was your mother's ticket out of here."

"Doris was too big for Baton, I guess," said Ellie.

"No, honey. But Baton was too small for her. There's a difference."

"Not much of one," called Poppy from his den.

"Don't pay any attention to him," whispered Nan. "He's an old grouch."

"He's mad because Doris is out again," said Ellie.

"Well, he'd like to see more of her. So would I. We'd like to see more of you and Marie and Albert, too."

"I wonder what will happen tomorrow," said Ellie. "After the callback."

Nan reached across the table and laid her old, leathery hand on Ellie's smooth one. "No sense in speculating," she said. "Leave tomorrow be. We'll find out soon enough."

*   *   *

"Where's my good-luck charm?" called Doris the next morning. "Come on, Eleanor. We have to be back at the theater in half an hour."

"Are you leaving already?" asked Albert. He emerged from the den wearing a black top hat. "You never saw our show."

"We're going to take turns being the assistant," added Marie. "When Albert is my assistant I'm going to make him wear Nan's high heels."

"Are not," said Albert.

"Am too."

"Well, I'll have to see it later," Doris told them. "I absolutely cannot be late for this. Ready, Eleanor? Here, take my script. You can read it with me in the car. I already have all my lines memorized, but I want to practice a few more times."

In the car on the way to Magnolia, Ellie read the three lines belonging to someone called Announcer over and over, while in between Doris recited Circus Girl's lines.

"So come on and join the Circus," Doris said as she nosed the Buick through the two blocks that made up the center of Baton.

Ellie wanted to say, "Doris, show me your school. Where did you go to school? Show me the drive-in where you said you saw *Laura*. Show me where your friends

129

lived. Is there a hospital here? Did you ever have to spend the night in it?" But she settled back in her seat and listened to Doris recite.

"Okay, one more time," Doris said when she had finished.

Ellie let a small sigh escape, then started the scene again.

ANNOUNCER: Hello, America. When you're tired, when you're hungry, when the kids are underfoot, when you just don't feel like cooking . . . where do you go?

CIRCUS GIRL: Why, to Circus, of course! Welcome to the home of family food and family fun! Where a complete meal costs less than a dollar, and the entertainment is free. That's right. While you wait for your food, you can ride the Circus Train, watch Boffo the Clown make balloon animals, and color the place mats. Children under twelve get a free box of Circus Crayons!

ANNOUNCER: And the food is fabulous.

CIRCUS GIRL: There's something for everyone. Circus Burgers, Happy Clown Hot Dogs, Acrobatic Onion Rings, steak, French Fries, and

even peanut butter and jelly sandwiches for
the kids.

ANNOUNCER: Or for the kid in you! And with our
new locations, the Circus is closer than ever.

CIRCUS GIRL: So come on and join the Circus!

"You know," said Ellie, "this commercial doesn't really make much sense. First of all, Circus is only in New York, so at the beginning, the announcer should say, 'Hello, New York,' not, 'Hello, America.' Because if you live in Idaho or somewhere you can't go to Circus. And also —"

"Eleanor, stop! Don't say anything else. You're going to confuse me," said Doris. "Please just read the lines."

"Okay," said Ellie. She paused. Then she added, "I think you're doing great, Doris. I really do."

"Thanks, hon."

"And I think you'll get this job. If you do, I'll bet we'll get to eat free at Circus from now on."

"Hon, if I get the job, we won't need to eat at Circus. We can eat at La Duchesse Anne anytime we want. Okay, let's try this once more."

"All right." Ellie cleared her throat. "Hello, America," she began.

*　　*　　*

This time when Ellie and Doris entered the Little Town Theater, the bored man at the door ushered them right inside.

"Now you go sit down, Eleanor," said Doris. "Sit where you sat yesterday, and keep thinking good thoughts for me, okay?"

"Okay," Ellie replied, and found her seat again. The silence in the theater that morning was, as Ellie had once heard David Levin's father say, deafening. Ellie crossed one leg over the other and jiggled her foot back and forth. She drummed her fingers on the arm of her seat as quietly as she could manage. And even while she told herself not to do it, she let her thoughts stray to Doris as the Circus Girl, to meals eaten at La Duchesse Anne (Ellie might even try snails), to climbing onto the school bus and calling hello to row after row of friendly faces.

Ellie, determined to think only happy thoughts, pretended that Doris had already been chosen the Circus Girl and that today's callback was actually a rehearsal. She straightened her back as the producer greeted the five returning women and asked them to sit in the front row and wait for him to call their names. She watched, feeling somehow detached, while the first woman walked onto the stage and read the scene with a young man who had been sitting next to the producer. She noted that the woman, who smiled and spoke very chirpily, left out the part about the Circus Train, and said, "Happy Clown Burgers and Circus Dogs," instead of, "Circus Burgers and Happy Clown Hot Dogs."

Ellie stiffened a bit as she watched the second woman, who didn't make a single mistake and was very beautiful. She wasn't quite as chirpy as the first woman, but she did smile a lot.

Ellie's confidence returned, though, when the third woman stumbled over her lines, started again at the beginning, stumbled a second time, and finally rushed through the rest of the scene, making it up as she went along. "That's right. Circus is happy to serve all kinds of food. Hamburgers and hot dogs and food just for the kids." She missed her last line completely, nodding and grinning when the announcer said that the Circus was closer than ever.

"Thank you, honey," said the producer after a short pause during which Ellie nearly jumped to her feet and called out, "So come on and join the Circus!" just to fill up all the empty air in the theater.

The producer looked at the man sitting next to him. Then, "Thank you," he said again. "You may go."

The woman put her hand to her mouth, walked quickly off the stage, and left the theater.

"Doris Day Dingman!" called the producer.

Ellie clasped clammy hands together, squeezed her eyes shut, then opened them. Doris stood on the stage, smiling at the man playing the announcer.

"Hello, America," said the announcer, and Ellie found herself silently reciting the rest of the line along with him. But when Doris began speaking, Ellie sat back and listened. From time to time she stole a glance at the producer. She saw him nod his head as Doris finally exclaimed, "So come on and join the Circus!" in a bouncy rhythm: So *come* on and *join* the *Cir*cus!

When the fifth woman began the scene and said her lines smoothly but way too fast, Ellie stopped listening. She turned toward Doris, who had taken her seat in the front row again, wanting to give her the thumbs-up sign, but Doris's eyes were fixed on the people onstage.

The producer thanked the fifth woman when she had finished. He scribbled on a pad of paper. He consulted with the man sitting next to him. He walked to the back of the theater and stood not far from Ellie in a dramatic pose, eyes closed, hands behind his back, taking deep breaths and turning his head upward as if silently consulting someone in the balcony. At last he returned to his seat. He eased himself into it. Then he stood up again and addressed the hopeful Circus Girls.

"This has been a difficult decision," he said. "Very difficult. But I can ask only one of you to remain behind. Wendy Johnson, Pamela Curtis, and Doris Day Dingman, you may go. Betty Creason, please come talk to me. You are our new Circus Girl."

Very quietly, Ellie got to her feet. She looked across the theater at Betty Creason, the beautiful woman. Betty had rushed to the producer and was squealing, "Oh, thank you! Thank you so much!" while Wendy, Pamela, and Doris gathered their coats and pocketbooks and made their way to the aisle.

Doris was the last to reach the aisle, and Ellie hurried to meet her.

"Doris!"

Doris Day Dingman, her eyes fastened on the back of the theater, walked stiffly behind Pamela Curtis.

"Doris?" said Ellie.

But Doris didn't answer.

On the way back to Baton, Doris swerved the Buick around corners and passed cars on narrow country roads. Ellie leaned cautiously to her left and peeked at the speedometer. The needle hovered near seventy.

"Doris," said Ellie tentatively, "you were the best one there. You really were. That producer doesn't know what he's talking about. He —"

"Eleanor," Doris replied quietly, "shut up."

Back at Nan and Poppy's, Doris stormed into the house and said only two sentences. "Eleanor, Albert, Marie, pack your things. It's time to go home."

"But —" said Albert, who was wearing the tall black magician's hat and Nan's high heels.

Ellie nudged him. "Don't argue," she whispered. "Just do what she says."

Half an hour later the Buick, with Doris and her things in front, and Ellie, Albert, Marie, Kiss, and their things in back, screeched away from Nan and Poppy's driveway. Ellie craned her neck around for one last look at her grandparents and saw them standing hand in hand on the front stoop, Nan holding a handkerchief to her mouth.

PART TWO

Bad Things

In early November of 1963, the weather in Spectacle grew unseasonably warm. Ellie and Marie started sleeping with their window open. Ellie missed the summertime night sounds — the crickets and katydids and peepers — but she breathed in the autumn smells and, when she had trouble sleeping, she let her mind wander ahead to the Harvest Parade — just two weeks away — and then to Thanksgiving and Christmas and anything that would take her out of school for a while.

One Saturday morning, after a particularly restless night, she awoke with a start when she heard a scream. She sat up, her mind foggy. Across the room, Marie's bed was empty. Light filtered through the curtains that fluttered by the open window. Ellie reached for her clock and peered at it, rubbing her eyes. Eight-thirty. She rarely slept this late. She listened for a moment but heard nothing. She must have been dreaming, she thought. And then she heard the front door slam and voices in her yard.

By the time she had tossed off her nightgown and

pulled on the clothes she'd worn the day before, which were lying on the floor, Kiss had begun barking.

"What is it? What's wrong?" Ellie called as she dashed outside, still barefoot. Her parents and Marie and Albert stood uncertainly in the front yard, looking down the street.

"Something at Miss Woods and Miss Nelson's!" Albert replied.

"I think it's a Bad Thing," added Marie.

Ellie, her feet freezing, because it was warm for November but not all *that* warm, jammed her feet into a pair of Albert's sneakers that she grabbed from the front porch. Then she pounded down the street, narrowly avoiding tripping over Pumpkin, who was flying along behind Holly. Ahead of her, the Witch Tree Lane families were gathering on the ladies' lawn.

"Who screamed?" Ellie asked Holly. "What happened?"

"I'm sorry!" Miss Nelson was saying. "I'm so sorry. Oh, I woke up the whole neighborhood."

"That's all right," said Mrs. Levin, putting her arm around Miss Nelson's shoulders.

When Ellie saw that everyone else — every single other person who lived on her street — was crowded around Miss Woods, who was standing defiantly by the Witch Tree, she let out a great lungful of held-in breath.

She wasn't sure what had happened, but no one seemed to be hurt, and so she sank to the grass and sat there for a moment. Ever since the afternoon when Doris had told Ellie to shut up, had wrenched her and Albert and Marie away from Nan and Poppy's, Ellie had felt doomed. It was why she couldn't sleep at night. It was why she jumped when the phone rang, why her heart pounded harder than usual each time the doors to the school bus swung open. Doris's mood had slowly improved since that awful day — and now all she talked about was the Harvest Parade — but Ellie had become jumpy. She didn't know what she thought might happen, just something bad.

And now, apparently, one of Marie's Bad Things had happened. Ellie's neighbors were peering at the Witch Tree. Ellie stood up on wobbly legs and looked at it herself. She saw that the knothole, the face of the witch, was a loud lavender color, and that drips of paint ran down the trunk of the tree.

Everyone was talking at once.

"This must have happened last night."

"Did anyone hear anything?"

"The tree is ruined."

"No, it isn't, dear."

"Can you get paint off of a tree?"

"I think it's spray paint."

"Should we call the police?"

"I'm so sorry I disturbed everyone."

Ellie stepped back from the tree, back, back, back until she was in the Levins' yard.

"Ellie? Are you okay?" Holly joined her, cradling Pumpkin in her arms.

Ellie nodded.

"Who do you think did it?" asked Holly.

Ellie shrugged. "Whoever does all these things. Someone who hates us."

"Monsieur Lauchaire is going to get some paint thinner or something," Holly reported as Pumpkin crawled up to her shoulders and settled himself around her neck.

"Is it okay to put paint thinner on a tree?" asked Ellie.

"I guess. Monsieur Lauchaire seems to think so. Gosh, Miss Woods is madder than a hornet."

Ellie looked across the yard at Miss Woods in time to hear her say, ". . . ought to have their heads examined. They have no respect for life. If I ever get my hands on them . . ." And then, "What's *wrong* with people?"

By lunchtime, the residents of Witch Tree Lane had resumed their weekends, but their mood was glum. Monsieur Lauchaire had scrubbed gently at the knothole with a rag soaked in something very smelly, and his cloth had turned purple, but the witch's face was still a faint violet color, and would remain that way for several years.

Miss Woods called the police, and was fit to be tied when the sergeant she spoke to said she was welcome to come down to the station to make a report, but that he didn't have time to drive all the way out to Witch Tree Lane to look at a purple tree.

"I ought to have *him* arrested," Miss Woods said that afternoon as she and Miss Nelson and Ellie and Holly sat on the ladies' front porch. "I could make a citizen's arrest."

"Oh, now," said Miss Nelson.

"Elizabeth, this is serious," Miss Woods went on. "Because when people do these kinds of things, well, it isn't the *things* that matter so much as why they do them. And they do them because they want to frighten us. They might as well come burn a cross in our yard."

"Dear!" yelped Miss Nelson. *"Please."* She inclined her head toward Ellie and Holly, and Ellie shivered and wrapped her arms around her chest. Next to her, Holly tightened her grip on Pumpkin, who was sitting in her lap. "Now you've scared the girls."

"Well . . ." was all Miss Woods would say.

Ellie's gaze drifted toward the defiled tree and the familiar old face.

*　　*　　*

That night Doris was jubilant. During the afternoon, while Ellie had sat shivering on the ladies' porch, Doris had gone into town for a meeting about the Harvest Parade. When she returned, she was the most cheerful she'd been since she'd gotten the callback for the Circus Girl audition.

"Just think!" Doris had exclaimed as the Dingmans sat down at their kitchen table for a supper of macaroni and cheese. "In two weeks I'll be riding through Spectacle as our Harvest Queen. It'll be my crowning moment."

Ellie giggled.

"What?" said Doris, looking at her sharply.

"You said your 'crowning moment.' Get it? Crowning?"

Doris frowned.

"It's a pun. Because you really are going to be crowned the Harvest Queen. So it's *literally* going to be your . . . never mind, Doris. It's great. You're going to be great."

Doris brightened. "I'm going to have my hair professionally done on Saturday morning. Early. Oh, and that reminds me. I have to make an appointment for the final fitting of my gown."

"Aren't you going to be cold wearing a gown outdoors in the middle of November?" asked Albert.

"Oh, no, hon. I'll be wearing a stole."

*   *   *

"A *fur* stole," Ellie added when she related this conversation to Holly the next afternoon. They had closed themselves into Ellie's bedroom, needing a moment of privacy. When Holly said nothing, Ellie repeated, "Fur. *Fur*, Holly. From some poor dead animal, but Doris doesn't care about that. . . . Holly? Holly? Yoo-hoo. Earth to Holly."

"Sorry," said Holly. "I was thinking about Mick. And how much I hate him."

Ellie slid off of her bed and sat cross-legged on the floor opposite Holly. "What did he do now?"

"He's just such a pig. He lies around our house wearing boxers and undershirts and nothing else and criticizes Mom when he finds the tiniest dust bunny on the floor. And then he'll ask her to do something like sew a button on his pants, only he *doesn't* ask, he orders. He walks up to her in his disgusting ratty undershirt and hands her the pants and says, 'These need to be fixed.' I have never heard him say please or thank you. And he only calls me 'Kid' or 'the kid.'"

"Maybe he never watched *Captain Kangaroo*," said Ellie.

The door to the room burst open then and Marie bounded in, followed by Rachel and Domi. "We're going to play house!" Marie announced. "Do you want to be our babies?"

Ellie smiled. "Well —"

"We were just leaving," said Holly, jumping to her feet.

"Darn," said Marie.

"But how about this: One of you could be the mother," said Ellie, "and the other two could be her twin babies."

"Oh! Yes! I claim to be one of the twins!" cried Rachel.

"And I am the other!" said Domi. "And our names are Pauline and Paulette."

"No, Annie and Frannie," said Marie.

Ellie and Holly escaped from the bedroom.

"Let's go over to my house," said Holly. "Mick's not there."

Outside, a wind had sprung up. It sent dry oak leaves rattling down Witch Tree Lane, and Ellie had the sudden thought that the warm weather was over and chilly November was here after all.

"Look, there's Pumpkin," said Ellie as she and Holly ran across the Majors' lawn. A small bundle of orange fur was sprawled on the front stoop. "Isn't it a little cold for him to be sleeping outside?" she asked.

Holly didn't answer. She stopped a few feet from the stoop and stared at Pumpkin. "Something's wrong," she said.

Pumpkin was lying on his side, feet stretched delicately away from him. His mouth was open, and so were his eyes, staring ahead. Ellie saw that he was panting, that his sides were heaving, and that a bit of foam had formed at the corner of his mouth.

Holly let out a shriek and then another and another.

The door to the Majors' house burst open. "Girls?" said Selena. And then she saw Pumpkin. She knelt beside him for a moment.

"What is it? What happened?" cried Holly.

"Maybe he was hit by a car," said Ellie.

"No," said Selena slowly. "I think he's been poisoned. I'll call the vet."

Ellie watched what happened next as if from a great distance; as if Holly and Selena and Pumpkin were putting on a play and Ellie were sitting in the last row of the theater. She watched Selena dash back into the house to make a phone call. She watched Holly sit on the stoop and cradle Pumpkin in her arms. She watched Selena return a few minutes later with a box lined with a blanket and lay Pumpkin carefully in it.

"Dr. Tierney will meet us in his office," Selena told Holly.

Then Ellie, who had backed away from the stoop, watched in silence as the Majors' car screeched out of the driveway, turned the corner, and disappeared down Route 27.

Slamming

Pumpkin had been poisoned. He died that night at the vet's office. Holly couldn't stop crying, and Selena didn't make her go to school on Monday.

On Monday afternoon, after two bus rides without Holly, during which Ellie had sat Allan in her lap and hugged him tightly, Ellie dragged herself to the Majors' house. Selena's car was gone, and Ellie found Holly staring at the television set, which wasn't turned on.

"Hi," said Ellie.

"Hi."

"I'm sorry about Pumpkin."

"I know."

"Dad said we have to keep Kiss indoors now."

Holly nodded.

"Does Dr. Tierney know how Pumpkin was poisoned?"

"No," replied Holly. "He said he could have eaten something, like fertilizer from someone's garage, but he wasn't sure. I can't really see Pumpkin doing that, though."

"Me neither. Holly? This is a really terrible thought, and I hope you won't get mad at me . . ."

"What?"

"Well, you don't think that Mick . . ."

"Poisoned Pumpkin?"

Ellie nodded.

"No," said Holly. "I really don't. I don't like Mick. And he doesn't like me very much. And he didn't like Pumpkin, either. But I don't think he killed him."

Ellie nodded again. "You know," she began.

"Yes. I do know," Holly replied.

And Ellie realized that Holly did indeed know exactly what Ellie was going to say. That if Pumpkin hadn't accidentally eaten poison, and if Mick hadn't poisoned him, then someone else, a stranger, must have set out the poison.

It was another of the Bad Things, only this time Ellie didn't think it could be called simply a Bad Thing, because it was so very horrible.

It seemed to Ellie that all that week the people of Witch Tree Lane kept to themselves. Selena cancelled several of her cleaning jobs so she could be at home with Holly more often. Mrs. Lauchaire and Mrs. Levin, who worked part-time, stayed home several afternoons as well. Even Doris stayed home more than usual. After school the children played indoors; no more tromping around up and down the street in a pack.

By Friday, Ellie was tired of being cooped up, playing house with Marie. "Come on, Kiss," she said. She fastened Kiss's leash to her collar and pulled her toward the front door. Kiss, who was used to running free, planted her feet firmly on the floor and rocked backward.

"Come *on*," Ellie urged her. "We're going to take a walk."

Kiss allowed herself to be tugged out the door and down the street to the ladies' house.

"Ellie!" Miss Nelson greeted her as she peeked through the front door. "And Kiss. What a nice surprise. Come on inside."

Ellie sat at the ladies' kitchen table, Kiss at her feet, while Miss Nelson bustled around and prepared afternoon tea.

When it was ready, Ellie and the ladies drank from china cups and ate tiny chocolate-covered biscuits. The ladies were quieter than usual, and Ellie, feeling pressed to come up with a topic of conversation, said, "How long have you lived on Witch Tree Lane?"

"Nearly twenty years," replied Miss Woods.

"Twenty years!" exclaimed Ellie. Somehow, she had never given much thought to what Witch Tree Lane had been like before *she* lived there. Now it occurred to her that other families had lived in her house, and in Holly's. She did remember, vaguely, other families who had lived in the Levins' and the Lauchaires' houses. But she couldn't even recall their names. She remembered a small boy — something had been wrong with him. What? Something with his heart. And she remembered a little girl who had a pet turtle that lived in a bean-shaped plastic bowl with a tiny plastic palm tree that offered no shade. And an older boy, a teenager, who zoomed up and down Witch Tree Lane in a car that made a lot of noise.

"What was our street like then?" asked Ellie. "Twenty years ago?"

"Oh, my, when we first moved here it was much different," said Miss Nelson. "For one thing, we were the only people on the street. Your house, and the other three, were built a couple of years after we'd settled in. So for two years the street was very, very quiet. Well, it's always been fairly quiet, I guess."

"Except for when that hideous Ronnie Marvel lived here," said Miss Woods.

"Was he the boy with the noisy car?" asked Ellie.

"Yes. I'm surprised you remember him."

"He used to honk and wave and yell things to Doris as he drove by."

Miss Woods rolled her eyes. And Miss Nelson said, "No one has manners anymore."

"Manners!" cried Miss Woods. "It's gone way beyond not having manners. People have no respect. This is a world full of hate."

"Oh, now, dear . . ." Miss Nelson's voice trailed off.

"That's why we're thinking of selling our house."

"Selling your house?" Ellie looked at the two old faces across the table from her. She set her teacup down and reached for Kiss, gulped in air.

"This is not the same little corner of the world it used to be," said Miss Woods. "There's a lot of judgment in this town. A lot of frightened, ignorant people. And when you take fright and add it to ignorance, you get hatred. That's a very unattractive equation."

"But, but . . ." sputtered Ellie.

Miss Nelson reached across the table and took Ellie's hand. "We're not *sure* we're going to sell the house. We're just thinking about it."

Ellie nodded, felt tears brewing, took a swallow of tea. "Dad says we have to keep Kiss indoors now. We can't let her run around outside anymore. I know she thinks she's being punished. It's not fair."

"A lot of things aren't fair," said Miss Woods.

Ellie looked outside at the darkening street. "I guess I'd better go home," she said. "Thank you for the tea."

*　　*　　*

The weekend passed — a dull, slow weekend with a sky the color of steel and a wind that thundered down Witch Tree Lane and tore the last few leaves from the trees. Monday and Tuesday passed in the same fashion, except that Ellie had the distraction of school. In school, if she concentrated very hard on her math or her reading book or Mr. Pierce's social studies project, she found that she could forget about Pumpkin, about the purple Witch Tree, about all the Bad Things and even the sparrows in the front row.

And then on Wednesday evening the phone rang at the Dingmans' house and a moment later Doris called, "Eleanor! Telephone!"

Ellie ran to the kitchen, where Doris stood holding the receiver toward her.

"It's not Holly," Doris whispered.

"Hello?" said Ellie.

"Ellie?"

"Yes?"

"Hi, it's Tammy."

"Oh! Oh, hi." Ellie pulled a chair out from the table and perched on it. She could feel her heart start to pound and told herself not to be silly. Why was Tammy calling her? She had more or less ignored Ellie since learning that Doris had not been chosen as the Circus Girl. Tammy was probably calling about homework. Although . . . if she had a question about homework, why wouldn't she call the other sparrows? Maybe she wanted Ellie to give her the answer to a math problem. Ellie was the best at math in their whole class, and everyone knew it. What should Ellie do if Tammy wanted an answer? She couldn't give her an answer. That would be cheating. Maybe —

"Ellie, listen, I want to tell you something and I don't have much time. I'm calling everyone in our whole class tonight. Except Holly."

"Except Holly? Why?"

"Because Nancy and Donna and Maggie and I decided that we should slam her."

"What — what does that mean?"

"It's something we used to do at my old school. You pick someone in your class and every time you pass that person in the hallway you slam into them. As hard as you can."

"You mean, to hurt them?"

"Or to make them fall down or something. It's funny."

"It doesn't sound funny."

"Oh, come on, Ellie."

"But why did you pick Holly? Why do you want to slam her?"

"Because she's, you know . . . weird."

"And you're calling everyone in our whole class?"

"Yup. I just have two more people to go."

"Is everybody going along with this?"

"Yeah. So you have to, too."

Ellie paused. "No, I don't," she said after a moment.

"What?"

"I don't have to go along with it."

"But I just said that everybody else is."

"I don't care. Holly's my best friend. Why would I do something like that to her?"

"Because she's *weird*. And if you don't go along with the rest of us, everyone will think you're weird, too."

"They already think I'm weird."

"Well, maybe you could change that."

"I'd rather be weird than mean."

Tammy didn't answer this, and Ellie did nothing to fill the quiet space. She twined the coil of phone cord around her finger and stared out the window. By the light of the lamppost in front of the ladies' house she could just make out the shadow of the Witch Tree.

"So you really won't slam Holly?" Tammy finally asked.

"No."

"Okay-ay," replied Tammy. "'Bye."

Ellie hung up the phone without answering her. She waited for just a moment, breathing hard, then picked up the phone again and called Holly.

"Do you think they'll really do it?" asked Holly as she and Ellie stepped off the school bus on Thursday morning.

Ellie sighed. "Yes."

"But do you think *everyone* will do it? Even Jimmy?"

Jimmy Bush was an unfortunate boy in the second row who picked his nose and talked about nothing but war planes. Most of the kids in Ellie's class left him alone; the sparrows weren't interested in him because he wasn't a girl. "I don't know," said Ellie.

"Well, do you think they'll just pick on me, like Tammy said? Or on you, too, because you wouldn't — "

"Holly, I don't *know*." Ellie felt cross with Holly, and knew she shouldn't, which made her even more cross.

"Well, how bad could it be, anyway? It doesn't hurt so much when someone bumps into you. Here, I'll bump into you right now." Holly leaned over and pushed Ellie to the side.

"*Quit* it," muttered Ellie.

"Sor-*ry*."

"Look, just don't say anything as we walk into school, okay?"

Ellie followed two fourth graders through the front doors of Washington Irving Elementary. She looked up and down the hall and saw no one from her class. "All right," she said to Holly. "Let's go."

The first kid who slammed into Ellie hit her so hard that she fell backward against a wall of lockers. She slid to the floor and waited to see what would happen next, but Maggie Paxton, laughing, only went on her way. She didn't even look over her shoulder at Ellie.

Holly, eyes bright, held out a trembling hand to Ellie. But before Ellie was on her feet again, WHAM. George Lott slammed Holly, who lost her balance and tumbled to the floor with Ellie.

This time Ellie held out her hand to help Holly to her feet. She looked around for a teacher, but saw only students.

WHAM. Anita Bryman slammed Ellie, raking her shoe down the back of Ellie's ankle.

By the end of the day, Ellie and Holly were bruised, Holly's knees were bleeding, and a bump was rising on Ellie's left shin. They huddled together on the bus.

"What should we do?" Holly whispered as the bus began to empty.

"Don't tell anyone," Ellie whispered back. "Not anyone at all."

They rode the rest of the way home in silence.

"I wonder how long you slam someone for." Holly said quietly to Ellie as they waited for the bus the next morning.

Ellie simply shook her head, mired in worry. She didn't think the slamming would go unnoticed for long. Sooner or later Albert would happen to be in the hallway when she or Holly was slammed. Or Marie would notice Ellie's scrapes and bruises. Or a teacher would see something. And any of these things, Ellie was certain, would only lead to much, much worse. Because the last thing a person wanted to do was get the sparrows in trouble.

At lunchtime, as Ellie and Holly hid behind a shelf of books in the library, their stomachs rumbling because they had avoided the cafeteria altogether, Holly said timidly, "Look, Ellie, I know you don't want to talk about this, but . . . I think we have to do something. My mother is going to want to know what happened to my dress." The seam of Holly's immaculate navy blue dress had ripped when Tammy had slammed Holly and she had caught her sleeve on the handle of a locker.

"Tell her you fell," said Ellie.

"Okay, but I'm going to be in trouble for that. This is a brand-new dress. And what about all these bruises? And my knees? Mom is —"

"Holly, forget it. We can't do anything about this. If our parents get involved, they'll call Mr. Pierce and he'll talk to Tammy and the rest of them, maybe even send them to the principal's office, and if that happens, believe me, everything is just going to get worse. Period."

"But —"

"Just wait awhile. We'll talk over the weekend, okay?"

"Okay."

"For now, let's go back to our classroom early. We'll skip the playground. I don't think anyone will notice. Then no one can slam us until the end of the day."

One more slamming opportunity — just one — and then the weekend. That's what Ellie was thinking when Mr. Pierce called her to his desk. Terrified that he wanted to talk about the slamming, Ellie was relieved when he simply handed her an envelope and asked her to deliver it to the principal's office.

Ellie slipped gratefully into the hallway, and in those few seconds before she noticed the first teacher crying, she experienced a moment of calm that she would remember for a long time — a small sense of peace that washed over her as she walked, unnoticed, through the halls of Washington Irving.

And then Mrs. Geary stepped out of her second-grade classroom, followed by Miss Riddel, the other second-grade teacher. Ellie saw tears running down Mrs. Geary's cheeks. As she wiped them away, Miss Riddel put her arms around Mrs. Geary, and Ellie saw that Miss Riddel was crying, too.

Startled, Ellie hurried by them. She passed a third-grade room, the door standing open, and saw three teachers in a huddle by the door. They were all crying, even Mr. Barnes.

Ellie quickened her pace. It must have been her imagination, but it seemed to her that the school had grown smaller and that the air was tight, as if the oxygen had been sucked out of it. She was nearing the principal's office when Mrs. Pazden, the school nurse, rounded a corner and ran into the teachers' room. Through the open door to the room, Ellie could hear a radio playing and saw a crowd of adults standing around it, staring at it as if it were a television. Two of them were facing Ellie. One gazed at the radio with a frozen expression, the other held a tissue to her eyes.

The principal's office, when Ellie finally reached it, was nearly empty. Only Mrs. Hale, one of the secretaries, was at her desk. The other desks, including Mr.

Taylor's in the room with the PRINCIPAL sign on the door, were empty. Ellie could hear another radio playing somewhere.

She wanted to ask Mrs. Hale what was wrong, since clearly something was very, very wrong, but when she handed Mr. Pierce's envelope to her, Mrs. Hale thumped it onto her desk and said briskly, "Hurry back to your classroom now, dear."

Ellie did as she was told, and walked through the hallways as fast as she could without actually running. She passed Miss Sachs, the gym teacher, whispering with Albert's teacher. She passed a fifth-grade classroom, the teacher perched on the edge of his desk, talking to his students. Ellie could see the students in the first row staring wide-eyed, like startled cats.

When she reached Mr. Pierce's room she turned the knob with a shaking hand, then jumped backward as Miss Pettig thrust the door open from the other side and exited with a whoosh of perfume. Miss Pettig had been Ellie's teacher in fifth grade and had written on Ellie's final report card that she was quiet, serious, and dependable, and Miss Pettig thought she could go far. "Reach for the stars, Ellie!" Now, as Ellie offered Miss Pettig a tremulous smile, Miss Pettig hurried away as if she hadn't even seen her, and knocked on the door of the next classroom.

"Ah, Ellie. Good, you're back," said Mr. Pierce, as Ellie stepped into the room. She thought she detected the slightest of wavers in his voice. "Please take your seat. I need to talk to the class."

Ellie, now thoroughly frightened, hurried to the back of the room. She was accustomed to giving a wide berth to Tammy, who sat at one end of the front row, but Tammy barely glanced at her. All eyes were turned toward Mr. Pierce.

"Boys and girls," said Mr. Pierce quietly as soon as Ellie was settled behind her desk, "I have something to tell you. Some bad news." He stopped speaking for a moment and let his gaze wander around the room, then out the window. "Our president — President John F. Kennedy — is dead."

Ellie felt something drain out of her then, although she couldn't have said what it was. Her hands and feet felt disconnected from her body, and she let out a small gasp, then covered her mouth, not wanting to attract the attention of the sparrows. But she needn't have worried. All around her were other gasps. And cries and exclamations. Tammy burst into tears. So did several other students, including Holly, who quickly put her hand to her mouth as though she could close off her tears that way.

Mr. Pierce began speaking again, still gazing out the window. "He was in Dallas," he said. "The president and his wife were in Dallas this morning. They were riding in an open car, and someone shot at him."

"You mean he was *murdered?*" cried Anita.

Mr. Pierce swallowed. "He died just a little while ago. The doctors tried to save him, but they couldn't."

Ellie expected a barrage of questions from her classmates. Is Jackie okay, or was she hurt, too? Did they catch the person who fired the gun? What happens now, now that our president is dead?

But the room had become absolutely silent.

Mr. Pierce glanced at the clock over the door. Ten minutes until the bell would ring signaling the end of the day. "Class dismissed," he whispered anyway.

Ellie looked around the room. At first her classmates didn't move. Then slowly they began to stir, replacing books in desks, removing sweaters from the backs of chairs, standing up. They filed wordlessly out of the room.

Ellie and Holly hung back for a moment, then followed the other students into the hall. The rest of the school must have been dismissed, too, Ellie realized, as the halls filled with silent children. Ellie had never been in the halls of Washington Irving Elementary when they were so crowded, and so quiet and orderly.

"I don't think we have to worry about being slammed," Holly whispered.

Ellie shook her head. "No," she whispered back.

When they were outside, the chilly air filling their lungs, Ellie saw that the school buses were still arriving, lining up in front of the school. "Let's wait here by the door," she said. "We'll watch for Allan and the other kids."

While they waited, they listened, catching snatches of conversation.

"He was shot in the *head*."

"The doctors couldn't save him; it was too late."

"When a president is murdered, it's called assassination."

"Think of Caroline and John-John. What are they going to do without their father?"

"My sister is the exact same age as Caroline."

Ellie and Holly watched the students streaming through the doors and grabbed Allan and the other Witch Tree Lane kids one by one. They sat together on the bus that afternoon, jammed three to a seat.

From the time the driver pulled away from the school until the first bus stop, not a word was spoken. The driver kept glancing in the rearview mirror at his silent riders. After the first stop (where, Ellie noticed, several mothers were waiting for their children), a few kids began to speak in hushed voices.

Allan, who was sitting in Ellie's lap, reached up, cupped his hand around her ear, and whispered, "What happens when you're dead?"

Ellie shifted uncomfortably in her seat and was still forming an answer when Allan cupped his hand around her ear again and whispered, his warm breath soft on her cheek, "Does it mean you don't get to have any more birthdays?"

"Well, yes," said Ellie, "but —"

"Why would someone want to kill President Kennedy?" asked David, turning around in his seat to face Ellie and Holly.

"A person *killed* him?" said Allan. "On purpose?"

"Maybe we should talk about this later," said Holly. And the Witch Tree Lane kids lapsed into silence again.

When they were the only ones left on the bus, when ordinarily they would have shouted and hooted and tried out mean nicknames, Allan said, "We're just going to be quiet today, aren't we?"

Ellie nodded, and the bus rumbled along Route 27.

When it stopped at the end of Witch Tree Lane, Ellie looked out her window and saw every single one of their parents — her father, Doris, the Levins, the Lauchaires, and Selena — standing by the stop sign. One by one, the children stepped off the bus, joined their parents, and walked to their homes.

The Longest Weekend

Ellie did not remember any weekend that seemed as long as the one that followed November 22, 1963 — not even the weekend when she was so sick with the flu that she couldn't read or even watch TV, could only lie in her bed with the shades drawn so the light wouldn't hurt her burning eyes or add to her pounding headache.

Doris flicked the television set on the moment the Dingmans walked through their front door. For a while Ellie and her family sat in the living room and stared at the black-and-white images before them. But Ellie grew tired of watching tearful newscasters, and eventually began to feel afraid.

She was just about to ask, "What happens to our country now?" when Doris stood up suddenly and, putting her hands to her cheeks, said in a loud whisper, "Poor, poor Jackie. A widow. A *widow*. Imagine. At her age. And with two small children to raise. Oh, the calamity."

Mr. Dingman turned away from the television, glanced at Doris, then turned back to the TV.

Ellie, still frightened not only by what was on the TV,

but by the very fact that all of the Witch Tree Lane parents had come home early in order to be with their children, wanted to go across the street to Holly's house, but felt numb, and drawn into her family as if they were her universe now. The five Dingmans sat in their living room, the TV playing in the background. Mr. Dingman read the newspaper, Doris painted her nails, Albert and Marie played Monopoly, and Ellie tried to read a book. They ate supper in front of the TV, the same news stories airing over and over, all the regular TV shows cancelled.

At eight o'clock the phone rang and Ellie leaped to answer it, expecting Holly. "Hi," said a male voice. "Is Doris Dingman there?"

"Doris, it's for you," Ellie said, and handed her the kitchen phone.

A few moments later Doris returned to the living room and turned down the volume on the TV. She stood before the rest of the Dingmans and said solemnly, "Well, it's happened."

"What?" Albert said in alarm, trying to see the television behind Doris.

"The Harvest Parade," said Doris, "has been . . . cancelled." She cast her eyes to the floor.

"Oh," said Ellie, feeling relief flood through her. "I thought someone else had been killed."

"And the parade won't be rescheduled," Doris went on. "This is it."

"Well, under these circumstances..." said Mr. Dingman.

"Oh, yes, yes. I know," Doris said quickly.

The Dingmans lapsed into silence.

That evening Doris was particularly quiet. She sat stiffly in her chair, only moving when she jumped up to change the channel on the television. Every time an image of Jackie Kennedy appeared on the screen Doris would sit down again and gaze at the First Lady, shaking her head and clucking her tongue. "A shame," Doris said more than once. "Such a shame." And, "All her dreams."

By Saturday morning, Ellie didn't think she could manage one more moment in front of the TV. Her father and Doris had taken their seats in the living room almost as soon as breakfast was over, Albert and Marie nearby, huddled over the Monopoly board.

But Ellie couldn't sit still. "Can I go to Holly's?" she asked.

"Oh, Eleanor, I don't know," said Doris, eyes on the screen.

"Please?"

"I think maybe you should stay at home. We'll have a quiet day."

"It isn't dangerous to leave the house, is it?" Ellie asked uneasily.

"No, of course not," said her father.

"Then can I please go? I don't want to watch TV all day."

"All right," said Doris. "Just don't make too much noise over there."

Ellie blinked. "Why not?"

"Because the *president* is dead."

Ellie didn't bother to phone Holly first. She grabbed her jacket and hustled out the door. As she was jumping off her front stoop she caught sight of David hurrying out of the Levins' house.

"David!" she called.

"Hi, Ellie! What are you doing?"

"Going over to Holly's."

"Can I come?"

"To *Holly's?*"

"I have to get away from the TV."

"Me, too. But I'll bet Mick has the TV on," Ellie said, eyeing Mick's car in the Majors' driveway.

"Well, let's do something."

Ellie and David convinced Holly to join them outside.

"It's so terrible," said Holly a few minutes later. She and Ellie and David had ambled to the end of the street and were now sitting on the frost-swollen ground, leaning against the Witch Tree, facing in three separate directions. "Mom says there's never been a president like Kennedy. I wonder what's going to happen now."

"The *vice* president takes over, dummy," said David.

"I know that. It's just . . ."

"Doris keeps talking about Jackie," spoke up Ellie. "She says she's a beautiful widow."

"That's weird," said David. "I mean she is beautiful, I guess, but . . ."

"I wonder what will happen to Caroline and John-John now," Ellie went on. She leaned her head against the trunk of the Witch Tree and looked up, looked at its bare branches spread across the gray sky, at the remains of an old nest resting sloppily on a branch.

"Well, they still have their mother," said Holly.

"Oh, yeah," said Ellie. "Right."

It was mid afternoon before Doris and Mr. Dingman finally got tired of the television. Mr. Dingman took Albert and Marie into town, and Ellie followed Doris around and around the house until finally Doris said, "Eleanor, don't you have something to do?"

Ellie had plenty to do. She had books to read, and homework, and the Extra List in her speller to study. But she was restless and felt the need to keep Doris in sight.

"I don't know," said Ellie. "What are you doing?"

Doris was standing in front of her closet, gazing into it the way Ellie sometimes gazed into the open refrigerator when she wasn't sure what she wanted to eat, or sometimes when she was just bored.

"I don't know, either," said Doris.

Ellie grinned, but Doris wasn't smiling.

"What's wrong?" asked Ellie.

Doris sank into the armchair. "I feel kind of bad about something."

Ellie's stomach turned over. "Bad? About what?"

"The parade. I wish it was still on. I wish I could still be the Harvest Queen. Is that very wrong of me?"

Ellie didn't think it was wrong, exactly, but she did think it was selfish. "Well . . ."

Doris waved her hand in front of her face. "I know, I know. Never mind."

Ellie lazily lifted one leg of her pants to scratch at a scab on her knee.

"Eleanor!" exclaimed Doris. "What did you do?"

Ellie glanced down at her bruised shin and hastily replaced her pants. "Nothing. I fell in gym."

"Well, try to be more careful."

In the next few moments Ellie found herself back in the halls of Washington Irving Elementary, felt herself being slammed from behind so hard that her breath was taken away, heard laughter, heard the sound of cloth ripping as Holly was slammed against the locker, heard Holly say, "I'm going to be in trouble for that."

Ellie breathed in, then let the air out slowly. Her heart began to pound. She felt as shaky as when she'd had to recite a poem in front of her whole class. "Doris?" said Ellie.

"Yeah?"

Ellie paused. "Nothing."

Sunday passed in much the same way as Saturday. And there was to be no school on Monday.

"Why?" asked Marie.

"Because tomorrow is President Kennedy's funeral. And burial," said Doris. "Everyone in the country wants to pay their respects."

On Monday the Dingmans once again gathered around their TV. They sat in silence as they watched the funeral procession pass through the streets of Washington, D.C. At the first sight of Jackie, Doris put her hand to her mouth and began to sob.

"Oh," she said. "Oh. Just look at her, her future changed forevermore."

"What about Caroline and John-John?" Marie said in a small voice.

Ellie looked at the Kennedy children in their tidy winter coats, standing solemnly beside their mother.

They looked so strong, all three of them. How could that be so? How could they be strong when their lives were falling apart?

Ellie felt tears prick at her eyes. She glanced at her father, saw him swipe the back of his hand across one cheek; looked at her brother and sister sitting motionless on the floor, eyes locked on the television. When John-John stepped forward and saluted his father's casket, Ellie had to turn away. Later, when the funeral was over, she said, "Will we have school tomorrow?"

"Yup," her father replied in a husky voice. "Back to school and back to work."

Back to normal, thought Ellie. Good. It was all she wanted.

Ghosts

At the bus stop on Tuesday morning. Ellie and Holly stood apart from the rest of the Witch Tree Lane kids.

"I'm in trouble for ripping my dress," said Holly. "Mom noticed it last night. She said if I want any new clothes before Christmas I'll have to buy them myself. And all I have is seventy-eight cents."

"Did she want to know *how* you ripped your dress?" asked Ellie.

"Yeah. I just told her I fell."

"Which is sort of true. You did fall."

"I guess." Holly looked thoughtful. "You know, all this — the slamming and my dress and everything — it's bad, but somehow it doesn't seem *so* bad after everything else that's happened."

"I know," said Ellie. "And, well, doesn't it make Tammy and the others seem kind of small? Compared to what happened to the Kennedys?"

Holly nodded. And the school bus appeared down Route 27, a yellow speck blooming into a great unwanted weed.

*   *   *

Later, Ellie and Holly hesitated outside the door to Washington Irving Elementary.

"Well?" said Holly.

Ellie looked at her watch. "We have to go in. If we don't go in soon, we'll be late."

"We never figured out what to do. I mean, if they keep slamming us."

"I know. I almost told Doris, but then I couldn't."

"That's okay."

"Ready?"

"Ready."

Ellie opened the door, and she and Holly stepped inside. The hallway was crowded and busy. And noisier than it had been on Friday afternoon when the students and teachers had left school feeling dazed. Still, something had changed. Ellie felt as if she were watching a movie with the volume lowered and the speed slowed down.

She glanced once at Holly, then began the walk to Room 12. When she saw Maggie Paxton approaching, she stopped and stiffened. Maybe, she thought, if running into Ellie or Holly were like running into a phone pole, the slamming would cease. But Maggie walked by as if she hadn't seen her.

"Huh," said Holly.

A few moments later, Anita Bryman hurried by them from behind. As Ellie and Holly watched her disappear into their classroom, Holly said, "Huh," again.

"Is it over?" whispered Ellie.

"Maybe they just want us to *think* it's over," said Holly.

Once inside Room 12, Ellie and Holly walked quickly to their seats. The sparrows didn't so much as look at them.

"Maggie, will you please take attendance?" said Mr. Pierce, handing Maggie his record book.

Maggie stood importantly in front of the blackboard, looking from the book to the students to the book again, making a column of check marks. Then she returned the book to Mr. Pierce.

Mr. Pierce glanced at it, then at Maggie. "I think you made a mistake," he said, frowning. "You marked Ellie and Holly absent."

"Yes," said Maggie.

"But they're here."

"Oh. I didn't see them."

Mr. Pierce shook his head and looked for an eraser.

During Language Arts, Mr. Pierce gave Richard Sutton a stack of composition paper and asked him to pass it out. Richard walked up and down the rows depositing one on every desk except Ellie's and Holly's.

Ellie raised her hand tentatively. "Excuse me, Mr. Pierce? Holly and I need paper."

"Richard?" said Mr. Pierce.

"Oh, sorry," said Richard. And when he reached the back of the room with two more sheets of paper, he whispered to the girls, "I didn't see you."

"We were right in front of you!" exclaimed Holly.

"What? Did someone say something?" Richard made a great show of looking around, as if he had heard a strange noise and couldn't find its source.

"I *said* —"

Ellie touched Holly's arm. "Don't," she whispered.

"But —"

"It's not worth it," said Ellie.

At lunchtime, the students in Room 12 put their books and papers in their desks and lined up at the door. As usual, Ellie and Holly hung back to stand at the end of the line. No sooner had they taken their places than Donna Smith ran back to her desk, rummaged around in it, and returned to the line. When she headed for the end, Ellie winced. And Holly whispered, "She's going to slam us as soon as we're in the hall."

But Donna didn't join the end of the line. Instead, she pushed her way between Ellie and Holly, stepping on Ellie's toes.

"Ow!" Ellie couldn't help crying.

"Oh. Didn't see you," said Donna.

In the cafeteria, Nancy and Tammy also didn't see Ellie and Holly, who were sitting in a back corner near the door. Carrying full trays, the sparrows walked to the table, and Nancy flumped down in Holly's lap while Tammy sat in Ellie's.

"Hey!" exclaimed Holly.

"Hmm. There must be something wrong with this seat," said Nancy. "Is anything wrong with yours, Tammy?"

"It does feel a little strange," agreed Tammy.

"*Get. Off,*" Ellie said quietly.

Tammy looked at Nancy with raised eyebrows. "Did you hear something? I almost thought I heard something. Like a voice. Or . . . I don't know. I guess it was nothing."

"Definitely nothing," said Nancy. "Ooh, look! Apple crisp." She picked up her fork.

Ellie, squashed beneath Tammy, Tammy's tray resting on Ellie's lunch bag, struggled briefly, then stopped, feeling rage gather somewhere deep inside. In the next moment she surprised herself by shoving Tammy to the floor and leaping to her feet, shaking. She might, she thought, even have taken a swing at Tammy.

But Tammy simply straightened her dress, stood up, looked across the table at Nancy, and said, "Gosh, these are weird seats. I think something's wrong with them. Let's move to another table."

When the girls had left, Holly, her eyes bright with tears, said, "Everyone's pretending they don't see us. It's like we're ghosts."

Ellie poked at her lunch bag with trembling hands. She realized that, in the practical sense, being humiliated was better than being slammed, and for that reason, she ought to feel relieved. Instead, she felt only the rage gathering again, and she fought hard to keep it at bay, to look at Holly, shrug her shoulders, and reach for her carton of milk.

Washington Irving Elementary closed at 1:00 on Wednesday for the start of Thanksgiving vacation. Four and a half entire days, Ellie thought, of being at home, where people could see her. So what if home was Witch Tree Lane, where Bad Things happened and the ladies were thinking of moving and no one knew who had poisoned Pumpkin. It was still home, and Ellie felt a little rush of hope as the bus reached the corner of her street.

When she hopped down the steps that afternoon with the rest of the Witch Tree Lane kids, Ellie was relieved to see Doris's car in the Dingmans' driveway. Good. That meant she and Doris could get right to work on Thanksgiving dinner. Doris had been so quiet and moody since Friday that Ellie hadn't dared ask her about cooking. Earlier, before last Friday, which, Ellie realized, seemed like years and years ago, she had thought of asking if maybe Nan and Poppy could come for Thanksgiving. But no one had so much as spoken about the holiday since the weekend. Maybe next year, Ellie had thought. Next year Nan and Poppy could come. For now, her hopes rose for at least a nice meal for the five Dingmans.

Ellie and Albert and Marie ran up their porch steps and inside their house, Marie calling, "Doris! Doris!"

No answer.

"Doris?" Marie called again.

"She must be upstairs," said Albert, and the Dingman children ran to their parents' bedroom to check.

No Doris.

"Well, the car's here," said Ellie. "Let's go back downstairs."

They found Doris in the kitchen, sitting at the table, the phone cradled between her ear and her shoulder, writing furiously on a small pad of paper.

"Doris! We didn't know where you were!" exclaimed Marie.

"Shh-SHHHH!" was Doris's reply. "I'm on the phone here."

"Excuse us for living," Albert said, and walked out of the kitchen, followed by Marie.

Ellie, now feeling crabby, dropped her book bag on the floor and stood by the table, arms crossed, facing Doris.

Doris continued writing. "Mm-hmm, mm-hmm, mm-hmm," she muttered. Scribble, scribble, scribble. "Mm-hmm. . . . When? . . . Okay." She glanced up and saw Ellie, then returned to her pad of paper. "Mm-hmm. . . . Just a moment, please." Doris cupped her hand over the receiver. "Eleanor, *what?*" she said.

Ellie looked pointedly from Doris to the John's Auto Parts calendar on the wall and back to Doris.

"What *is* it?" said Doris.

"Tomorrow is Thanks*giv*ing," Ellie said in a loud whisper, although she didn't know why the person on the other end of the phone shouldn't hear her say this.

"Eleanor, please. I'll be off the phone in a minute."

Doris returned to her conversation, and Ellie opened the refrigerator and surveyed the contents. Suddenly she felt slightly sick. She saw a package of bologna and another of cheese. She saw an open container of milk and a slice of meat loaf in Saran Wrap. There were a few other things, too — ketchup and mayonnaise and grape jelly and half an apple. But where was the turkey?

Where was the apple pie Doris always bought at the A&P? Where were the potatoes?

Ellie closed the refrigerator and opened a cupboard. No cans of corn or peas or aspic. No jars of olives or pickles. Quietly she closed the cupboard and turned around to face Doris again, just as Doris said, "Okay, thank you. 'Bye," and hung up the phone.

"Um," Ellie said, not sure what to be more nervous about — the fact that she had interrupted Doris's phone conversation, or the fact that Doris was completely unprepared for Thanksgiving. "I thought you might have gone to the grocery store today." And then a thought struck Ellie. Maybe Doris was waiting for the Dingman children to come home so they could all go to the store together.

"I know," Doris said vaguely, looking at her notes. "I meant to." She slipped the pad in her pocket.

"Well?" said Ellie.

"Well, what?"

"Thanks. Giv. Ing. You know, getting a turkey? Cooking?"

"Oh, Eleanor, I'm just not up to all that this year." Doris paused, then put on a broad smile. "I had a great idea this afternoon. We're going to have Thanksgiving dinner at the Starlight Diner. Won't that be fun?"

"The Starlight Diner?!" cried Ellie. "Will they even be open?"

"Yes. I checked. Won't that be fun?" Doris said again.

"Who goes to a diner for Thanksgiving?"

"Lots of people."

"Have you told Dad yet?"

"I'm going to tell him tonight."

Doris Needs a Vacation

Mr. Dingman, after a moment of tense silence, said he didn't mind Thanksgiving dinner in a diner, but Ellie could tell he was as disappointed as she was.

"I know!" Ellie said brightly that evening. "If it's because you don't want to do all the work, Doris, then the rest of us can do it. I understand. It's a big job. Why should you have to do it every year? This year you can be on vacation, and we'll cook the meal." She turned to her father. "We could do it, couldn't we? Couldn't we, Dad? I can cook."

"That's a nice idea, Ellie, but I'm afraid it's too late for that now." Mr. Dingman looked stiffly at Doris over his reading glasses. "The stores are closed. Anyway, I'm sure dinner at the Starlight will be fun."

Ellie turned miserably to Doris. "Is it because you need a vacation?" she asked. "Is it because Albert and Marie and I don't do enough around here? We can do more. I'll talk to Albert and Marie."

"No," said Doris. "It's not that. I just wasn't up to it this year, what with the parade being cancelled and

President Kennedy and poor Jackie and her half-orphan children and all." She paused. "Well, maybe I *could* use a vacation. But not because of you kids. You're great, the best. Now why don't you go on upstairs and figure out what you and Marie are going to wear tomorrow."

Ellie didn't think it mattered what they wore to the Starlight, but she went upstairs, anyway.

The streets of downtown Spectacle were quiet on Thanksgiving afternoon.

"Wow, where is everybody?" Marie said as Mr. Dingman steered the Buick toward the diner.

"They're at *home*," said Albert, "watching TV and smelling the turkey cooking."

"Albert," said Mr. Dingman. "No more of that, please."

Albert slumped even lower in his seat, then edged to his right until he was pressed against Marie's side.

"Quit it!" said Marie.

"What'd I do?"

"You touched me."

"Albert," said Mr. Dingman again. "What did I just say?"

"Well, what are you going to do to me? Take me home? I don't *want* to go to the stupid diner."

Mr. Dingman glared at Doris, but she was staring out the window.

"There's a parking place!" she exclaimed. "And look. It's right in front of the diner."

"What a surprise," muttered Albert.

Ellie reached across Marie and swatted Albert's knee. "Be quiet," she hissed.

"You're not the boss of me," said Albert, but he got out of the car without further comment.

The Dingmans were dressed in their holiday clothes. Albert and Mr. Dingman were wearing suits and ties, and Ellie had polished their shoes that morning. Marie and Ellie were wearing matching dresses that Doris had found at Korvette's — sleek, satiny blue fabric with wide lace collars and large sashes tied in bows in the back. Ellie felt she was much too old to be wearing this type of dress, but figured no one from her class would be in the Starlight, so she didn't care. Doris was wearing a very tight emerald green suit that she'd been offered at a reduced price after modeling at Harwell's, a white blouse with an enormous bow at the neck, and many, many bangle bracelets. Her piled-up hair was adorned with green combs, and she had done something with curlers that created loose ringlets around her ears.

"My, my," said Doris as the Dingmans reached the door to the Starlight. "Just look at us. All gussied up. Hon, this is such a treat," she added, turning to Mr. Dingman as if Thanksgiving at the diner had been his idea.

Mr. Dingman didn't answer her. He opened the door, to which was taped a cardboard turkey with brilliantly colored tail feathers, and held it impassively as Doris, Ellie, Albert, and Marie passed inside ahead of him.

"Gosh, what a crowd," muttered Albert, looking around.

The diner wasn't deserted, but Ellie had never seen so few people in it. And she had hardly ever been so conscious of herself and her family as she was at that moment. When Mr. Dingman opened the door, a bell above it rang. And every single person in the diner turned to see who had entered.

Ellie scanned the faces as they studied her. She counted twelve people. One was the cook, two were waitresses with sparkly turkey pins fastened to their uniforms, and nine were other diners. Three of the diners were seated at the counter, each alone, separated from the next person by at least one empty stool. Three elderly couples were sitting in small booths, which were decorated with cardboard pilgrims and cornucopias and droopy orange crepe paper. Nobody was saying much. And nobody was nearly as dressed up as the Dingmans were.

"This is depressing," Albert whispered to Ellie.

"I know," she whispered back. "But let's not make it worse than it is."

One of the waitresses stepped out from behind the counter, grabbing a stack of menus on her way.

"Happy Thanksgiving!" she said gaily as she approached the Dingmans. Ellie read the waitress's nametag. LORNA.

Marie's face lit up. "Happy Thanksgiving!" she replied.

"Where would you like to sit? Take your pick. You can have any of the big booths," said Lorna.

The Dingmans chose a booth at the back of the Starlight. When they were seated, Lorna handed out the menus. "We're featuring our regular lunch selections," she said. "Plus, we also have the Thanksgiving Special. A meal with all the trimmings for one low price. It includes a full turkey dinner, consommé to get you started, a side salad, pumpkin pie for dessert, coffee for the adults, and milk for the kids."

Doris didn't even open her menu. "My!" she exclaimed. "That sounds delectious." Ellie felt Albert nudge her under the table. "And what a bargain!" She glanced around at the rest of the Dingmans. "I think we'll have five specials. Right?"

"But I don't want consommé," said Marie.

"Is consommé sticky?" asked Albert.

Doris laughed nervously. "Now, now. Let's remember our manners. We're in a restaurant. If you don't want something, just say you don't care for it."

"I don't care for consommé," parroted Marie and Albert.

Lorna made some notes on her pad, returned the pad to her pocket, on which was pinned the sparkly turkey, and left the Dingmans, saying, "I'll be right back with water and your free rolls."

"Now," said Doris, looking around the diner, "I know this isn't, what do you call it, a traditional Thanksgiving, but it's very nice, isn't it? We get a complete dinner with all the trimmings."

Ellie was watching her father. She saw him determinedly put a smile on his face, and realized that he wanted to save the holiday, to take Doris's lemons and make lemonade. He loosened his grip on the edge of the table and smiled around at his family. "You know what? You're right. This is a treat," he said.

"It's so sad, though," said Doris.

Mr. Dingman let out an enormous sigh and stopped just short of rolling his eyes.

"What is?" asked Ellie, as Albert said, "The Starlight?"

"I can't help wondering what Jackie is doing today. Her first Thanksgiving without her husband. This isn't what she planned." Doris paused. "Whoosh."

"What?" said Marie.

"Whoosh," Doris repeated. "In one instant . . . Jackie's entire life . . . changed." Doris's eyes filled with tears. "I can't stop picturing John-John saluting his father's casket," she went on. "Every time I close my eyes I see that. And Jackie, so brave. And of course, the president. His life cut short. A true tragedy."

Ordinarily, Ellie would have listened to such talk with half an ear, but now she glanced up sharply. Something in Doris's voice made her uneasy. She looked at her father and saw that he, too, was watching Doris.

All during the Dingmans' dinner — during the consommé and the side salads and the turkey and the slices of pumpkin pie — Ellie considered Doris. She remembered Doris on the phone the day before, and Doris watching the president's funeral, and then for some reason the memory of Doris's face when she lost the part of the Circus Girl. And by the time the meal was over and the stuffed Dingmans were thanking Lorna and filing out the door, Ellie knew that something was very, very wrong. She just didn't know what it was.

On Friday morning, Mr. Dingman left early to go to work, thankful to have a cold-weather job transforming the basement of someone's house into a rumpus room.

And the Dingman children, even Ellie, slept late. Eventually, Ellie was wakened by the sound of their front door closing, and was shocked to see that the hands on her clock pointed to nine-fifteen. She scrambled out of bed, and when she heard a car engine kick to life, she rushed to the window. There was Doris backing the Buick down the driveway in a big hurry.

Shopping? wondered Ellie. Groceries? Definitely groceries, she decided, remembering what was in the refrigerator.

Ellie stumbled downstairs and set three places for breakfast.

It was after Ellie and Albert and Marie had eaten both breakfast and lunch that day and were beginning to think about dinner that Albert said, "Where is Doris, anyway?"

"I'm not sure," replied Ellie. "She left this morning just as I was getting up. I thought she was going to the grocery store."

"What time did you get up?"

"Nine-fifteen."

Albert looked at the clock. "That was seven hours ago."

"Maybe she had an audition," said Marie. She was sitting on the kitchen counter licking peanut butter off of a Ritz cracker. "Or a lesson or something."

The Dingman children were used to being at home alone, but usually they knew where Doris was.

"Maybe you should call Dad," said Albert.

"I don't think Doris left his phone number," said Ellie. "And I don't know where he's working today. Anyway, he'll be home soon. In an hour or so. I have an idea. Let's surprise him with a nice dinner."

Albert whipped the refrigerator door open, then closed it with a bang. "A nice dinner of cheese and grape jelly?"

"Oh, come on, Albert. Be creative." Ellie removed a can of hash from the cabinet. "See what's in the freezer, Marie," she said.

"Dad, where's Doris?" Albert asked the moment Mr. Dingman returned.

Mr. Dingman walked into the kitchen, brushing sawdust out of his hair, and looked at the table set for four, a candle burning in a china holder. A smile crept across his face. "What's all this?" he asked.

"Dad, where's Doris?" repeated Albert.

"What?"

"She's been gone all day. We don't know where she is."

"And we didn't know how to call you," added Marie.

"I'm sorry, honey," Mr. Dingman said, pulling Marie into his lap. "I gave the number to your mother."

"Well, from now on, maybe you should give Ellie your numbers," said Albert.

Doris hadn't returned by the time Ellie went to bed that night. Nervous, knowing that her father was nervous, too, Ellie lay awake until nearly midnight, listening for the sound of the Buick in the driveway. She remembered years ago, when she was younger than Marie, lying awake on Christmas Eve, listening for the sound of Santa on the roof — of sleigh bells jingling, of reindeer hoofs pawing the snow.

Ellie turned over and listened instead to Kiss snoring lightly at the foot of her bed, and to Marie's gentle breathing.

Doris had not returned when Ellie awoke the next morning. And her father had not gone to bed. Ellie found him in the kitchen, stirring up a cup of Sanka, wearing the clothes he'd had on the day before. His shirt was untucked, his hair was uncombed, and his face was unshaved.

"Shouldn't we call the police, Dad?" Albert asked later as the Dingmans stood around the kitchen sink eating Cap'n Crunch.

"I don't think so."

"Why not?"

"I just . . . don't think it's necessary."

"When will it be necessary?"

"Don't push me, Albert."

The Buick returned at 3:22 that afternoon. Albert waited by the front door and pounced on Doris before she could even set down her pocketbook.

"Where were you?" he demanded.

Doris unbuttoned her coat very slowly and very carefully. As she hung it in the closet, she said, "I had to get out of the house."

"That's it? You had to get out of the house?"

"I'm in no mood, Albert. Leave me alone."

Everyone left Doris alone. Ellie knew Doris had something to say, and she didn't want to hear it.

Life Is Short

Doris spent most of Saturday evening in her room, the door closed. The rest of the Dingmans watched television in silence. Once, Mr. Dingman left the living room, went upstairs, and knocked on the bedroom door.

"Hon?" he called. Ellie couldn't make out Doris's reply, but it was very short, and then Mr. Dingman said, "Okay," and returned to the TV.

Ellie was surprised to awaken on Sunday morning to a chipper Doris bustling around the kitchen, the table set for five, a plate of doughnuts in the middle.

"Wow!" said Ellie. "Where did these come from?"

"I went to the bakery," replied Doris. "Now go on and wake up your brother and sister. Let's have breakfast together."

Ten minutes later, the five Dingmans, some of them groggy, were seated at their kitchen table. Doris wore an apron and walked around the table, serving doughnuts as if she were Lorna the waitress.

"Isn't this nice?" she said.

Ellie looked out the kitchen window at the dreary day. A fine drizzle was falling, and a mist had set in. She peered at the thermometer outside the window. Forty-two degrees. And she shivered. But she had to agree that sitting around the kitchen table with her family, a plate of doughnuts, and Kiss leaning against her legs, was very nice indeed.

"It's great," said Marie, her mouth full of chocolate doughnut. "Can we have doughnuts every morning?"

"Well, hon, I don't know about that. I guess it will be up to your father."

"Up to Daddy? Why?" asked Marie.

"Yeah, why?" echoed Albert.

Before Doris answered, before any words left her mouth, Ellie felt her own mouth go dry. She set her half-eaten doughnut down on her plate and looked all around the kitchen — at the cupboards with the chipped green paint, at the plate shaped like a fish that had been hanging over the doorway for as long as she could remember, at the section of counter between the oven and the refrigerator that the Dingmans called the Messy Corner — but she couldn't look at Doris. Ellie let her eyes drop to her plate again, to the remains of the doughnut, and waited for Doris's answer.

"Why?" repeated Doris. "Well . . . because — because of my exciting news!" Doris pushed her chair away from the table. She stood up and began to speak. As she spoke, she moved around the table, standing behind each of the Dingmans in turn, her hands on their shoulders. "I've been doing a lot of thinking," Doris said. "That's where I've been the last couple of days. I needed to think."

"I can think in our house," said Albert.

Doris removed her hands from Albert's shoulders and leaned around to look into his eyes. "Well, I couldn't," she said. "Not about this."

She moved on to Marie. "It's hard to know where to begin."

"Begin at the beginning," said Marie, tipping her head back and smiling at Doris.

And Ellie thought, She doesn't know. Marie doesn't know that this is bad news.

"It's even hard to know where the beginning is," said Doris. "I think the beginning was a long time ago. Maybe before you were born. But the thing is . . . what I've been thinking about . . ." Doris drew in a deep breath and moved on to Ellie. "The thing is . . . life is short."

Ellie, ignoring Doris's hands on her shoulders, glanced across the table and saw Albert roll his eyes.

"Life is short," Doris said again. "That's what I realized when President Kennedy was killed."

Ellie now glanced at her father and thought his eyes looked brighter than usual.

"The president's life was cut short and Jackie's was changed forever," Doris continued. "There were probably lots of things both of them wanted to do that they won't be able to do now — all their plans and dreams. And so I realized that you never really know how long you have. Which reminded me that if you want your dreams to come true, you have to *make* them come true. You can't just sit around and wait for things to happen.

"That's why," Doris continued, "I have decided to go to New York City to pursue my dream of becoming a star."

"*What?*" cried Albert.

"Can I go with you?" asked Marie.

"No, dummy," said Albert. "She doesn't mean she's taking a trip. She means she's leaving us. Don't you, Doris?"

"You're deserting us," Ellie whispered.

"I am not *deserting* you," said Doris. "I'm paving the way for your future."

Ellie glanced at her father again. He had not said a word since Doris began speaking. And now Ellie saw that, as Doris stood behind him and placed her hands on his shoulders, he crossed his arms and rested his hands on hers, his face rigid except for trembling lips.

"I don't understand," said Marie.

"Me neither," said Albert.

"Well, try," said Doris, exasperated. "Look. This is what I've been thinking. There are lots of things I can do in Spectacle, like modeling at Harwell's and acting in community theater. But I'm not going to get my big break here, and if I have to go somewhere else to get my break, then I better go now, while I'm young."

"How long will you be away?" said Marie in a small voice.

"I don't know, hon. Probably for a while. This is going to take some time. I'll have to find an apartment and get an agent. And then I'll take on whatever acting jobs I can find. I'll be prepared to do anything — commercials, more modeling, bit parts, anything. Now's my chance to get on *The Ed Sullivan Show*. Or maybe one day I'll be in a soap opera. Just think if I could get a part in a soap! That could pay really well. But I need to get established."

"And then what?" asked Ellie. "What happens after you're . . . established?"

"Then I send for you!" said Doris triumphantly.

"All of us?" asked Marie.

"Of course all of you."

"You mean we'll move to New York City?" asked Albert.

Doris grinned. "Just think of the life we could lead, living in the big city. We'd have a great huge, deluxe apartment. Maybe we'd have a view of the Empire State

Building out our windows. Each of you would have your own bedroom. No more sharing. And you kids would go to one of those fancy schools where you wear a uniform. And we'd have a maid and a cook."

"Right," said Albert.

"Well, it could happen," said Doris.

In the movies, thought Ellie.

"Anyway, it's what I want for us." Doris sat down again and reached for a doughnut.

Mr. Dingman cleared his throat, but nobody said anything.

"Well?" Doris put on her perkiest face. "What do you think?"

Ellie tried to imagine living in a New York City apartment. She thought of apartments she had seen on television. There was the Ricardos' apartment on *I Love Lucy*, but it wasn't very fancy. In fact, it was smaller than the Dingmans' house. She had seen some pretty fancy apartments in the movies, though. Apartments with doormen, and butlers who walked rich ladies' dogs, and . . . an image of Ann Miller's lavish apartment in a movie called *Easter Parade* sprang to Ellie's mind. Then Ellie pictured the sparrows perched in the first row of desks in her classroom, and recalled being slammed into lockers and marked absent in the attendance book. And *then* she pictured the school bus pulling up at the corner of her street, her hopping off the bus with the other kids, tea parties with Miss Woods and Miss Nelson, sharing secrets with Holly, and looking into the face on the Witch Tree.

Maybe Doris knew what she wanted, but Ellie didn't.

"Doesn't anybody think *any*thing?" said Doris.

"When are you going to leave?" Marie asked finally.

"Pretty soon, I guess. Why waste time?"

"Since life is so short," said Albert. He placed his elbow on the table, rested his chin in his cupped hand, and stared at Doris until she looked away from him.

Ellie could think of about a thousand questions. Everything from *Are you taking the Buick?* to *Where are you going to get the money to live in New York City?* But two questions rang loudest in her head, over and over, like the bonging of great church bells: *Why don't you want to be our mother anymore?* and *How will Dad take care of us when you're gone?*

She hoped her father would ask these questions, though, and, head lowered, she slid her eyes over to him. But Mr. Dingman was staring down at his plate. Ellie wanted to grab him by the shoulders and shake him. Say something! she wanted to shout. Do something!

"Isn't anyone excited about living in New York City?" asked Doris.

Please don't do this to us, thought Ellie.

"Can we play in that big park?" asked Marie.

"Central Park? Sure, every day!" replied Doris.

"Can we at least finish school here this year?" asked Albert. "I don't want to be the new kid somewhere in the middle of the year."

Ellie once again looked to her father. Her head was buzzing, and for a moment she was sitting at her desk in Mr. Pierce's room and Doris was walking through the door to her class, interrupting the spelling quiz. Ellie willed herself back to the present. She waited for her father to lose his patience with Doris, to push away from the table in a rush and say, "You can't leave this family. I forbid you to go." But he was silent, and his face was as flat and as unexpressive as the knothole on the Witch Tree.

"Of course you can finish school here," said Doris. "I think it will take me a while to get established. That's why I want to leave right away."

Doris flew around the house like a tornado that day. She cleaned. She organized a closet. She made notes and lists of things for Mr. Dingman and the Dingman children to do after she was gone.

"Doris?" said Ellie that afternoon.

Doris was pulling pot covers and dish cloths out of the Messy Corner. "What, hon?"

"Can I help?"

"With this? No, I think it's a one-person job."

"But I *could* help around the house more, you know. Maybe you really do just need a vacation. I talked to Albert and Marie and we decided we could do all the cooking. We already make our lunches for school, and we could make breakfast and dinner, too."

"Hon, that isn't the point."

"Plus, we could do the cleaning. I know you get stuck with most of that. And the laundry. I could learn to do those things. Then, see, if you had more free time, maybe you could just take little trips to New York sometimes. Instead of moving there."

"That's a very nice offer, Eleanor," Doris said as she reached into the farthest recess of the Messy Corner with a damp sponge, "but I won't get as much accomplished if I do that. I need a protected period of time in New York."

Ellie glared at her mother, "Pro*tract*ed," she said, once again feeling rage gather inside her, in some deep and secret place. She stalked out of the kitchen.

Later, near dinnertime, Ellie found her father seated at the small desk in the living room, his checkbook open and a pile of bills before him. She hadn't heard her parents say one word to each other since they had left the breakfast table that morning.

"Dad, do you think Doris will be gone long?" Ellie asked, peering over his shoulder at the little pile of envelopes that was growing by his adding machine.

"I don't know."

"Well, do you think she'll really be gone until we finish school this year?"

"I don't know," he said again. "Probably."

"And then what?"

"I don't know."

"*Dad.*"

Mr. Dingman finally turned around and looked at Ellie. "Honey, the thing about your mother is that she has to try these things. She gets ideas in her head and she just has to carry them out. Harwell's never had a fashion show before your mother came along, right?"

"Right," said Ellie.

"And now she wants to move to New York City. Everyone should be able to follow their dreams, shouldn't they?"

"Well, why can't she be happy here with us?" Ellie cried, and she kicked at the leg of the desk before turning her back on her father and running to her bedroom.

When Doris finished straightening out the Messy Corner, which Marie said would now have to be called the Neat Corner, she went to her room and set her largest suitcase on the bed. First Marie, then Ellie, and finally Albert followed her into the room. They lay on the bed in a row, Ellie and Albert on the ends, Marie in the middle.

"Remember when we watched you get dressed the day you got your Bosetti Beauty crown?" said Marie to Doris.

Doris smiled. "I certainly do," she replied. She opened the suitcase, then the top drawer of her dresser.

"We watched you just like this," Marie went on, and Ellie saw Marie's chin quiver.

"Except then you weren't leaving us," said Albert.

Yes, she was, thought Ellie.

Doris faced her children. "I know this is hard," she said.

"Not for you," Albert said, and shot a rubber band across the room. It snapped into a perfume bottle, knocking it to its side.

Doris righted the bottle. "Yes, it is hard for me."

"But you're going to do it, anyway."

"Yes." Doris began to lift an enormous pile of clothes out of the open drawer. She looked at the pile, set it down, looked at Ellie and Albert and Marie. "Why don't you kids run along now? See if your father needs you for anything."

Albert and Marie slid off the bed and left the room. Ellie rolled to the edge of the bed, but lingered there.

"You sure are taking a lot of things with you," she said.

"Well, I'm probably going to be gone pretty long. And my apartment might not have a washing machine in it. I don't want to spend all my time sitting around laundromats."

"Are you going to miss us?"

"I'm going to miss you very much."

"How will we know where you're staying?"

Doris sighed, sounding impatient, so Ellie slid to the floor.

"I'll write as soon as I'm settled."

"Okay," said Ellie. As she reached the hallway she heard Doris say, "This is going to be the adventure of a lifetime."

PART THREE

Postcards

On February 10, 1964, Marie Curie Dingman turned eight, a FOR SALE sign was pounded into the yard in front of Miss Woods and Miss Nelson's house, and Ellie looked over her calendar and realized that it had been seventy-seven days since she had last spoken to Doris. Ellie hadn't expected this. She had known Doris was going to be gone a long time, but she had envisioned lengthy evening phone calls during which Doris would chatter on and on about her apartment, her auditions, her agent, and the famous people she had met.

Also, Ellie had thought Doris would call on Marie's birthday. Marie thought so, too, of course, and had even refused to go to the Starlight for a birthday supper because she didn't want to miss the call. The phone did ring twice. The first time it was Rachel Levin, who had just seen Marie an hour earlier, calling to sing a birthday song she had made up. The second time it was Nan and Poppy, which thrilled Marie. But when Mr. Dingman announced that it was bedtime (he insisted on early bedtimes on school nights) and Doris hadn't called yet, Marie burst into tears and told her father he was a stupid-head.

"It's still time for bed," said Mr. Dingman.

"I hate you," Marie replied, and slapped Kiss's nose on her way upstairs, for which Mr. Dingman swatted Marie, and Marie slammed the door to her bedroom, threw herself onto her bed, and sobbed.

Later, when Ellie tiptoed into the dark room, Kiss at her side, and quietly turned back the covers on her bed, she heard quiet sniffling.

"Marie?" said Ellie. "Are you still awake?"

No answer.

"You know, I'm sure Doris was thinking of you today," said Ellie.

"Then why didn't she call?"

"You know why. Because she doesn't have a phone."

"But why couldn't she call me on a *pay* phone?"

Ellie didn't have an answer for that. She thought, in fact, that her father and Doris conducted late-night phone conversations. Four times now she had been wakened from a deep sleep to the sound of the phone ringing, then had heard her father's muffled voice, sometimes raised, sometimes lowered, on the other side of her bedroom wall. But Mr. Dingman hadn't said anything about these calls, and Ellie hadn't asked.

*　*　*

The Dingman children had received only postcards from Doris. They were never dated. The first one, with a picture of the Empire State Building lit up at night, had arrived on December 12, almost two weeks after Doris had left. It was very hard to read. Marie thought Doris might have written it while riding on a New York City subway. Ellie had spent a long time studying the card and finally decided that it said:

> *Here I am in Gothim! Very, very exiting. No aprt*
> *yet am staying at ladies hotel. Looked at one apmt*
> *this morning no good. Looking at 2 more this aft.*
> *Love to all of you!!!!!*

"At least she's having fun," Albert said as he tossed the postcard in the kitchen garbage pail.

The second postcard arrived on December 23 and was very fancy. It was a painting, not a photo, of a cardinal perched on the branch of a fir tree. Snow dusted a pinecone and the tips of the cardinal's wings, and was sparkly with glitter. The card simply said:

> *Merry merry Christmas darlings!!!!! The city*
> *gloes at the holidays. I think I have an apmnt.*
> *Love and kisses!!!!!!!*

One afternoon, sometime after the first postcard arrived and about a week before the second one arrived, Albert stomped onto the school bus, glowering. He stomped by Etienne, with whom he usually sat, and flung himself down into an empty seat, glaring so fiercely at anyone who approached him that even the nastiest of the bus riders left him alone. Ellie asked him three times what was wrong, and each time he ignored her, staring pointedly out the window.

"You have to tell me sometime," she said as they let themselves into their house later.

"Fine," Albert replied. He opened his grubby note-book and withdrew a sheet of lined newsprint, which had been stapled to a piece of red construction paper. On the newsprint was a letter Albert had written in careful cursive. The letter was tidy, except for the first line. Ellie had a feeling that this line had originally read, "Dear Mom and Dad." But Albert had erased the words "Mom and" with such vigor that he had created a large hole between "Dear" and "Dad." Bits of pink eraser still clung to the edges of the hole. "We're learning about friendly letters," Albert said, jamming his hands in his pockets, "and Mr. Franklin said we should write Christmas letters and they should start with 'Dear Mom and Dad.'"

"Oh," said Ellie, suddenly understanding. "And Mr. Franklin doesn't know Doris is in New York."

"No." Albert examined the letter, rubbing his finger over the hole. "We're supposed to give these things to our parents, but I didn't want to give mine to Dad the way it was before. And now I can't give it to him like this." He crumpled it up, threw it in a wastebasket, and stalked out of the living room.

Marie looked at Ellie. "I want to write to Doris," she said.

"But she doesn't have an address yet."

Marie stuck out her chin. "But I want to write to her."

"But we *can't.*"

"But I *WANT TO!*"

"I know you do."

"We haven't seen her in so long. It's been so many days."

Ellie sighed.

"And it's almost Christmas. Maybe she'll have an address soon. Let's make her Christmas cards. Please, Ellie? Can't we make her Christmas cards? We should send her *some*thing. She might not get any presents this year."

"Well . . . that's a nice idea," Ellie replied slowly. "Okay. I'll make her a card, too. I guess we can send them later."

Ellie stood at the bottom of the stairs and called to

Albert that she and Marie were going to make cards for Doris.

"So what?" he replied, and slammed his bedroom door.

Ellie just managed to put together a Christmas for Albert and Marie that year. Mr. Dingman gave her some money, and on December 21, two days before Doris's second postcard arrived, Miss Nelson drove Ellie downtown and Ellie did the Christmas shopping for her family. She bought a skirt, a game called Sorry!, and a new Bobbsey Twins book for Marie. She bought a sweater, a baseball, and a Hardy Boys book for Albert.

"Doris used to do all the Christmas shopping," Ellie said to Miss Nelson as they left the bookstore.

"And now you're doing it."

"The wrapping, too. Dad doesn't really have time."

"But what about —" Miss Nelson stopped herself. Then she asked, "Do you have a tree yet?"

Ellie shook her head. "I think we're getting one tonight, though."

Miss Nelson looked at the gray sky. "Snow!" she exclaimed. "We'd better go get some hot chocolate. That's what you have to do when it snows."

At the Starlight, Ellie and Miss Nelson sat side by side in a booth, Ellie's packages piled on the seat across from them.

"You know," Miss Nelson began once Lorna had taken their order, "if there's ever anything you need, all you have to do is call Miss Woods or me."

Ellie stared into her glass of water, suddenly very tired. "We don't need anything."

"But if you ever do —"

"If we ever do, we'll ask Dad," Ellie snapped. "Anyway, you're going to move."

"We might not," said Miss Nelson. She spread her paper napkin in her lap. "No matter what, I want you to know we're here."

Ellie, looking across the table at the packages, felt small and mean. Miss Nelson had given her fifty cents in the bookstore, when Mr. Dingman's Christmas money had run out.

Ellie rested her head on Miss Nelson's shoulder. "What if I needed you every second?" she asked.

"That would be okay."

On Christmas Day the Dingmans opened their presents quietly. Ellie tried to make the morning cheerful. She put *21 Christmas Favorites* on the record player. And she was surprised and pleased to find a few presents under the tree that she hadn't bought herself, including one with a tag marked FOR ELLIE. Inside was a black velvet dress, just her size — and nobody knew where it had come from.

"Are all these presents from Santa?" asked Marie, who didn't believe in Santa anymore, although she said she did.

"Most of them are," said Ellie quickly.

"Santa's handwriting looks kind of like yours."

Albert and Marie had taken a great interest in the mail in December. They knew as well as Ellie did that nothing but the two postcards had arrived from Doris. But there was always hope. And if Ellie said some of the presents were from Santa, well, who knew who might have sent them.

On January 2, school began again and two postcards arrived from Doris. She had scrawled a large #1 on the one with a picture of Central Park, and a #2 on the one with a picture of a horse pulling a carriage along a tree-shaded path.

"Why doesn't she just write us a letter?" asked Albert.

"Maybe she only has postcard stamps," said Marie.

The #1 postcard said that Doris had finally found an apartment. *It doesn't have a phone, but heres my address.* The address, on West 55th Street, took up the rest of the card.

The #2 postcard read:

> *I have an agent!!!!! My own agent!! He's already booked me on three jobs I'm on my way!! New Years eve very gala.*

"I wonder what she did on New Year's Eve," said Marie.

"I wonder if she wonders what *we* did on New Year's Eve," said Albert.

Marie considered the postcards. Finally she said, "So she has an agent, an apartment, and three jobs. Ellie, does that mean she's . . . what is it she has to be before we move to New York?"

"Established?" said Ellie.

"Yeah. Is she?"

Ellie looked at the postcards again herself and shrugged. "She doesn't say how big her apartment is. And I don't know how many jobs you have to have before you're established. Probably not yet, Marie. But she's on her way."

"Huh," Albert said, and slammed the refrigerator door closed. "I'm going to Etienne's."

"I'm going to Rachel's," said Marie.

Ellie opened the refrigerator and scanned the dismal contents. She wrote herself a note to remind her father to go to the grocery store on Saturday. Then she snapped on Kiss's leash and ran across the street to Holly's house.

"Don't come in!" Holly exclaimed, meeting Ellie breathlessly at the front door. "Mom cleaned the house for Mick this morning. She doesn't want anything to mess it up."

"We won't mess it up," said Ellie.

"Kiss's fur! Kiss's fur!" cried Holly. She was shrugging into her winter coat. "We'll have to sit out here and talk." She paused. "Or go over to your house. Is there anything to eat at your house?"

"We have pretzels," said Ellie. "One bag of pretzels. That's it."

Holly made a face.

"When is Mick coming over?"

"Tonight. Mom is planning a fancy dinner, all this food I'm not allowed to touch. I don't know why she bothers. Mick is just going to criticize everything and then Mom will cry and they'll fight and Mick will say he's going home, but first he'll tell Mom he needs money and she'll cry some more but finally she'll give him some and he'll jam it into his pocket like she *owes* him, and then he'll leave."

Ellie looked at Holly and sighed. Then she looked down Witch Tree Lane at the ladies' house and their mailbox that had been bashed in with a baseball bat on New Year's Eve. She looked up at the dull gray sky, at a row of juncos perched on a telephone wire, which made her think of the sparrows, and she put her head down in her arms and cried.

Lies

Between January 2 and Marie's birthday, one more postcard arrived. It was a rather uninteresting shot of a taxicab and read: *Audition today for broadway play!! They need girls who can sing dance and act.*

"Do you think she'll get to be in the play?" Marie asked Ellie.

Ellie considered this. "Well . . . she can act."

Marie's birthday came and went. Marie was thrilled with the cake the ladies baked for her — it was in the shape of a giant sunflower — but Ellie had no idea what to say when Marie asked why Doris couldn't call her on a pay phone.

On Witch Tree Lane, the ladies bought a new mailbox, and this one was bashed in late the next Saturday night. A rock was thrown through the living room window of the Levins' house. And Ellie guessed that Kiss, whose belly now swayed slightly when she walked, had gained a good three pounds from being cooped up in the Dingmans' house all day long.

In school, Ellie and Holly continued to be ghosts —

ignored, overlooked, stepped on, and left behind, by every single one of their classmates. Unless they were being silently tormented.

"I didn't think it would last this long," said Holly.

"Me neither," said Ellie.

"At least they're not slamming us."

Ellie didn't answer. In the girls' changing room before gym class that morning, Tammy had waited until Ellie had slipped off all her clothes except her underpants, then had grabbed Ellie's gym suit and thrown it on top of the lockers, leaving Ellie standing mostly nude on the chilly tile floor. Ellie had crossed her arms over her newly swelling breasts and tried not to cry while Holly, still in her jumper and blouse, had leaped up and down, up and down, until she was able to sweep Ellie's suit to the floor with a ruler.

"Tell Miss Sachs," Holly whispered to Ellie as the rest of the girls ran giggling into the gym.

"What good would that do?" Ellie had replied. She scrambled into the suit, which was now grimy with dust. "Tammy will just say, 'I didn't know it was Ellie's gym suit. I saw it lying on the floor and I thought someone lost it.'"

"I still think we should tell Miss Sachs," said Holly stubbornly.

But Ellie shook her head.

Tammy White was now the unchallenged leader of the sparrows. Maggie, Nancy, and Donna did whatever she said, and looked to her before making any decision. And if there had ever been a possibility that Ellie would regain the shred of status she had once held with Tammy, that had disappeared when Doris left Spectacle, an event every Spectacular now knew about.

When Ellie returned home from school that day, carrying her gym suit so that she could wash it, she and Albert and Marie found another postcard from Doris.

"It says she got a job," exclaimed Marie. "I wonder if it's the one in the Broadway play."

"Don't know," replied Ellie, who, after tossing a load of clothes into the washing machine, retreated to her bedroom with the postcard. Albert and Marie had taken Kiss to the Lauchaires', and Ellie had the house to herself. She looked at the photo of Times Square on the card. She tried to picture Doris's apartment. She thought of New York City with its millions and millions of people, not one of them Tammy. In fact, there was not a single person in all of New York who had ever heard of Eleanor Roosevelt Dingman. Except her mother.

"Dad?" said Ellie that night after the Dingmans' supper of hamburgers and frozen lima beans, neither of which Marie would eat.

"Hmm?" Mr. Dingman was sitting at his desk in the living room, frowning at a stack of papers, which Ellie supposed were bills.

"Can I go visit Doris in New York?"

"What?" Mr. Dingman tossed the papers aside and removed his glasses. "What?" he said again.

"Can I go to New York? To visit Doris?"

"By yourself? Of course not."

"Please, Dad. I really want to. I need to see Doris." Ellie didn't add that she also needed to escape from Spectacle.

"But Ellie, you can't travel to New York alone."

"Then let's all go. Vacation is coming up. The first week of March."

Mr. Dingman paused, cleared his throat, and said, "It's a nice idea, Ellie, but . . . we can't afford it."

Ellie had been thinking about this conversation all afternoon, and she was prepared. "Wouldn't you like to know what Doris is doing?" she asked. "She has a whole life down there in New York City."

Mr. Dingman's eyes darted briefly to the darkness outside the window before he said, "We still can't afford to go."

"So let me visit her by myself."

"Ellie! Absolutely not," said Mr. Dingman. "That's the end of this discussion."

Ellie had other ideas, and they involved telling a lot of lies, but she didn't care. She was desperate.

The last day of school before vacation was a Friday. On Wednesday afternoon that week, Ellie sat on Holly's stoop, running the tip of her rubber boot through the slush that had accumulated on the Majors' front walk. "Holly?" she said. "On Monday, do you think you could take care of Albert and Marie all day? I'll pay you three dollars."

"What?" said Holly. "Why? What are you going to be doing?"

"I just feel like I need a little break. All I do is go to school, do my homework, take care of the house, take care of Albert and Marie. I'd like one day when I could just, you know, spend the whole day reading in the bathtub. Without being bothered. You could invite them over to your house to make fudge or something."

"Well, all right. But what if they get bored and want to go home?"

"Huh." Ellie hadn't thought of that. "Okay, then," she said after a moment. "I know. There are special programs going on at the library all week, because of vacation. Do you think your mom could drop you and Albert and Marie off at the library on her way to work Monday morning? And pick you up at the end of the day? She would understand if you said I needed a break, wouldn't she?"

"I guess so."

"And she'd like the idea of your spending the day at the library. Very educational."

"What *is* going on at the library?"

"I don't remember exactly," said Ellie. "But I'll find out. Everything sounded like fun."

That night, Ellie sat at the kitchen table, her math homework spread in front of her. She tried hard to concentrate on the questions about angles and degrees. But her mind kept straying to her closet and the things hidden at the back of it: her packed suitcase and her broken piggy bank, which was actually a Siamese cat bank. Despite the fact that the bank had once been a present from Holly, Ellie had smashed it with a hammer and removed all her money from it — wads of crumpled dollar bills, which she now knew were enough to buy a round-trip ticket to New York City.

Ellie's lies had been told, her plans were in place.

Gotham

On Friday afternoon, the students in Ellie's class were restless. A single hour lay between them and nine days of freedom. Earlier, Ellie had been not just restless, but panicked: Holly had not come to school. Ellie had spoken to her on the phone the night before — but she had not appeared at the bus stop in the morning. What had happened? Was she sick? What if she couldn't take Albert and Marie on Monday? Worse, what if Holly's mother suspected something?

At lunch, Ellie had used her ice-cream dime to call Holly from the pay phone in the school lobby.

"What's the matter? Are you all right?" she had squeaked when Holly answered the phone.

"I just have a cold," said Holly. "I already feel better."

Ellie breathed a sigh of relief. "Okay. I'll come see you after school."

Now it was almost the end of the day, and Ellie's classmates were fidgeting and wiggling and whispering.

"Okay, kids," said Mr. Pierce as he closed his copy of the sixth-grade math book, the one with the answers to the problems written in red ink. "I know it's hard to concentrate. I have an idea. Put your books away and let's talk about what we're going to do over vacation. We'll go row by row, starting with you." He pointed to Maggie. "This will be an exercise in public speaking," he added. "When it's your turn, please stand by your desk, speak clearly, and keep your comments brief and to the point."

Ellie thought for a moment. Holly wasn't here, and when Ellie walked out the door of Washington Irving Elementary, she wouldn't see or hear from a single person in her class until school started again. She could say anything at all about her vacation plans.

Ellie realized that her heart was not pounding, her hands were not sweating. In fact, she was almost sorry she was in the back row and would have to wait so long for her turn. She listened impatiently as classmate after classmate stood and talked about sleeping late, visiting grandparents, playing with brothers and sisters. When Tammy said grandly, "My parents said I could get a new record player," Ellie had to stop herself from snorting.

Finally, after what seemed like years, Mr. Pierce said, "Okay, Ellie. Your turn."

Ellie rose and said proudly, "I will be going to New York City, traveling there by myself." She looked across the room and saw that although Tammy was still facing the blackboard, her back had stiffened. "My mother has an agent now and is in a Broadway play, so I'll be going to the theater every night and eating dinner with other actresses and actors. Of course, I'll also get to go to the Statue of Liberty and the Empire State Building and Central Park. I'll be leaving on Monday, and I'll be gone the rest of the week."

Ellie sat down again and looked smugly at the row of sparrows. She was staring at the back of Tammy's head when Tammy turned around slowly, caught Ellie staring at her, reddened, and faced front again. Later, when school was finally over, Ellie sat cleaning out her desk while her classmates gathered their things and ran gleefully for the door. A shadow fell across Ellie, and she glanced up. Tammy stood over her. She offered Ellie a smile.

"Are you really going to New York?" she asked.

Ellie gazed around the room, trying to look perplexed, then murmured, "That was so weird. I thought I heard someone say something. But I guess it was nothing." She stared at Tammy for a moment, as if looking through her. "Yup. Definitely nothing."

The first weekend of vacation passed slowly. The weather was chilly and gray and rainy, and Mr. Dingman, who had had fewer jobs than usual lately, seemed content to sit around the house for two days. He assured Ellie, though, that he would be starting a new job on Monday; that in fact he would have to leave early to get to the job site on time. Ellie was relieved, and hoped this also meant that he wouldn't be home before dinner that night.

On Monday morning Ellie awoke at five, even though her bus didn't leave until close to one. She lay in bed and tried to recall everything she had learned about New York City. She'd needed a lot of information — such as where the bus station was and where Doris's apartment was and the general layout of the streets. Ellie had visited the library and found maps of New York and books about Gotham, and had studied and read until she felt familiar with the area of New York encompassing the bus station, which she learned was called the Port Authority, and West 55th Street.

At six, Ellie heard her father get up, and he left the house by six-thirty. Perfect. By nine, Ellie had sent Albert and Marie across the street to the Majors', bag lunches in their hands as if they were going to school. A few minutes later she watched Selena back her Ford station wagon into the street, and she counted heads to make sure four people were in the car.

As soon as the car had disappeared down Route 27, Ellie began rushing around her house. She cleaned. She made piles of sandwiches and left them in the refrigerator. She wrote notes reminding Marie and Albert and her father to take the garbage out, to bring the mail in, to feed Kiss (but to remember that Kiss was on a diet), and to keep her water bowl full. An image of Doris flying around the house on the Sunday after Thanksgiving came into Ellie's head, but she erased it quickly.

At eleven, Ellie called the Royal Taxi Company for a ride to the bus station, and by twelve-thirty she was standing at the ticket window, her suitcase at her feet, purchasing a round-trip ticket to New York City. She told the clerk that she would be traveling by herself but that she would be met in New York by her mother.

"All right," replied the clerk. "You'll have a stop in Kingston, but don't get off there. Stay in your seat. New York is another couple of hours from Kingston."

Fifteen minutes later, Ellie's adventure began. The bus to Kingston arrived, and she took a seat directly behind the driver, thinking how nice it was to board a bus without all the other passengers staring at her and holding their noses. Ellie's suitcase was stowed in the belly of the bus, and she felt light and free, nothing to keep track of except her book bag, and the money that was stuffed into her coat pockets.

Gears grinding, the bus pulled away from the curb and chugged along King Street. Harwell's and La Duchesse Anne and the Starlight Diner and

Washington Irving Elementary fell away as Ellie left Spectacle behind.

For a while, Ellie simply looked out the window. The bus wound through small towns, through the countryside, along barren roads dotted only with auto parts stores and gas stations. She was just about to dig her new Nancy Drew mystery, *The Password to Larkspur Lane*, out of her book bag, when the woman sitting next to her said, "Are you traveling alone, dear?"

Ellie knew she shouldn't talk to strangers, but she didn't really see how she could avoid it. For one thing, she would have to talk to a cab driver when she arrived in New York, and he (Ellie assumed all cab drivers were he's) would be a stranger.

And now here was her seatmate, a stranger, asking her a question. Ellie couldn't very well ignore the woman, could she?

"Yes," said Ellie. Then, to be polite, she added, "Are you?"

The woman laughed. "Well, I guess that's a fair question. Yes. I'm traveling alone, too. I'm on my way to Kingston to visit my sister."

The woman was old, older than Miss Nelson or Miss Woods. And she was so frail, her skin so papery, that she looked as though she could vanish in a little puff of smoke at any moment.

"I'm on my way to visit my mother," said Ellie.

"To visit her?"

Ellie nodded. "She's in New York City, getting established."

"Oh . . ."

"As an actress," added Ellie.

"I see." The woman looked as though she didn't see at all, and also as though she might have a lot more questions.

"Have you ever read a Nancy Drew book?" asked Ellie, who was in no mood to start explaining Doris.

"Why, no, dear."

Ellie didn't stop talking about Nancy Drew until the bus had pulled into Kingston.

At the depot, Ellie helped the woman off of the bus, then returned to her seat. She was relieved when no one else sat next to her, and she spent the next two hours reading, napping, and poring over the one map of New York City that she had brought with her. She was silently rehearsing what she would say to the cab driver who would take her to Doris's apartment, when to her left she saw rising above the horizon a collection of tall buildings. They appeared so suddenly that she gasped. As the bus drove on and the city loomed closer, Ellie could pick out familiar buildings, ones she had seen in the books at the library.

Ellie was gawking out her window when the bus turned sharply to the right and, before she knew it, was trundling through a dim tunnel. After several minutes she saw a pinprick of light ahead, and when the bus emerged into the late afternoon, Ellie found herself in a canyon of bricks and cement and granite.

"Gotham," she said under her breath.

The bus turned several corners, then drove inside a massive building and trailed through a labyrinth of dark passages until it squeaked to a halt and the driver opened the doors and stepped off the bus. Everyone else on the bus rose and started impatiently down the aisle. Ellie joined them. She reached for her suitcase as the driver unloaded it, and was startled when a man stepped in front of her to grab his suitcase first. Then she followed the other passengers through a doorway into a lighted area.

What was this? A waiting room? Ellie had no idea. It was full of people, most of them in a hurry, the rest of them standing in long lines. She looked around and, at last, after spotting a sign that said EXIT, rode up an escalator like the one in Harwell's. At the top, Ellie found herself in a room that was similar to the one below, but even larger and more crowded with bustling people. However, ahead of her she saw doorways and a sidewalk, and beyond that a street with cars and buses and yellow taxicabs. She could hear the blare of horns. Ellie lugged her suitcase to the doors and stepped outside.

New York City spread before her.

"Don't gawk," Ellie reminded herself. "Don't look like a tourist. Look like you belong here."

But Ellie was sure she was gawking anyway, and she couldn't help it. The city was just so . . . busy. She saw flashing signs and moving cars and hurrying people, and heard shouts and backfires and bells ringing, and smelled hot dogs and exhaust and something steamy and sour that she couldn't identify. And so, for a moment, she stood on the sidewalk and turned in a tight circle, looking up, up, up until she was dizzy. All around her towered buildings taller than any in Spectacle. Ellie felt like a chipmunk on the forest floor.

She didn't know how long she might have stood there, on the sidewalk outside the Port Authority, but someone bumped into her from behind (and didn't bother to say "excuse me"), and she remembered what she had to do.

Clutching her suitcase with one hand, and a five-dollar bill with the other, Ellie stepped to the curb, saw a yellow cab about to drive by her and, just as if she were in a movie, she put one arm in the air and called, "Taxi!"

The taxi swerved toward Ellie, so that she had to jump aside. When it stopped, she opened the back door, shoved her suitcase onto the seat, climbed in after it, and gave the driver Doris's address as she had rehearsed it on the bus.

The driver said nothing, just jerked the cab back out into the traffic. Ellie was riveted to her window. She gripped the armrest and stared outside as more shops and people and cars and baby carriages and dogs on leashes than she could imagine whizzed by. She watched the street signs, too, and was relieved to see that the numbers were rising. Very soon they were passing 53rd Street. Then the driver turned off the busy avenue and into a quieter neighborhood. Here were fewer stores and more trees, and row after row of low buildings, all connected, each with a short flight of steps leading from the sidewalk up to a doorway.

"Here you go," the driver said suddenly, pulling up next to one of the flights of steps.

Ellie paid the driver. As the cab sped away she stood on the sidewalk, looking for the Buick. When she couldn't find it, she turned and gazed up the steps at the number painted over the doorway. Doris's address.

Ellie was standing outside Doris's New York City apartment.

55th Street

The steps to Doris's apartment building were made of some kind of brown stone and were crumbling. Ellie climbed them carefully. When she reached the top she tried the door, unsure what to expect. She had never been to an apartment building before. The door opened, and Ellie entered a vestibule. Another door was before her, and beyond that was a flight of stairs leading upward. On one wall of the vestibule was a column of buttons, and next to each was a slip of paper with a name and number printed on it. The newest-looking piece of paper read DORIS DAY — 3B.

Ellie looked at the buttons. She looked at the door before her. Maybe the buttons were doorbells. Ellie pressed the one by Doris's name. She heard nothing. She waited for several moments. She pressed the button again. Nothing. She looked at the cracks running down the dirty walls of the vestibule, at some grease marks on the glass doors, at dust and a wad of hair and lint in a corner. Ellie became aware of a familiar but unpleasant odor, which eventually she decided might be urine.

She considered pressing the button again, but instead reached out and tried the door ahead of her. It opened, and Ellie, surprised, grabbed her suitcase and walked inside.

3B, she thought. Where was 3B? She could see two doors, one at the foot of the stairs, one across the hall from it. Ellie peered at them. One said 1A and the other 1B.

"Oh," Ellie said aloud, and began to climb the stairs. The stairs were dark. She passed two lightbulbs that had burned out. At the second floor, she stopped and looked down the hallway, which was dingy and smelled vaguely of cooking oil and food — scorched coffee, roasted potatoes, and the pungent, swampy odor of old fried fish. When she reached the third floor she walked quickly to the door marked 3B and looked for a bell. She didn't see one, though, so she rapped on the door.

The hallway was silent.

Ellie rapped again.

Nothing.

"Doris?" called Ellie. "Doris?"

Ellie set her suitcase down.

She knocked once more, called "Doris?" once more, then sat on her suitcase. She looked at her watch. Almost 5:15. Doris must be acting in her Broadway show. Ellie wished she knew which show it was so she could find it and surprise Doris when it was over. Ellie sat for five minutes, then looked at her watch again.

Back in Spectacle, Holly's mother would probably be picking up Holly and Marie and Albert at the library. Or maybe she had already picked them up. Ellie hoped her father would be home by the time Albert and Marie got back. If no one was there to greet her brother and sister, Holly's mother might be worried. Well, that hardly mattered, Ellie realized. When Ellie didn't show up in a reasonable amount of time, *everyone* would be worried. What would happen? Probably the grown-ups would talk to Holly, ask her if Ellie had said anything about what she wanted to do on her day off. Holly would think hard, remember Ellie saying something about taking a bath. Everyone would try to recall the last time they had seen Ellie. Finally, someone might suggest calling the police.

The police. Ellie pictured the worried faces of her family, felt her father's fear. She swallowed. What had she done? Maybe she should try to find a pay phone and call her family. But she didn't want to leave her post.

Ellie heard a door slam below, and she leaned over the railing to look down the stairwell. She saw nothing, but heard the sound of footsteps on the stairs, then a key turning in a lock on the second floor, then another door closing.

Half an hour later, Ellie had nearly decided to find a pay phone after all when she heard more footsteps on the stairs. These footsteps continued climbing until a head appeared at the top of the stairs opposite her. The head belonged to an old man, white hair in a crew cut that stood straight up from his scalp, his face pale and wrinkled. He grunted as he passed Ellie, then climbed the steps to the fourth floor.

Ellie checked her watch for what seemed like the two thousandth time — 5:52. She stood and stretched, stiff from sitting on the suitcase, and realized she heard footsteps on the stairs yet again. Ellie listened to the steps as they climbed to the second floor, and then the third. She watched the staircase, waiting for a head to appear as the old man's had.

The first thing she saw was a black velvet hair ribbon. Under it was lightly teased blond hair, then the top of a pair of sunglasses.

Ellie leaped to her feet. "Doris!" she cried.

Doris jumped, then gripped the banister to keep from falling. She let out a gasp. "Eleanor!" she exclaimed. "What on *earth?*"

"Surprise!" said Ellie. "I'm here for a visit!"

For just the smallest fraction of a second, Doris's face registered surprise, alarm, and then dismay. "What?"

"It's — we're having — it's school vacation. You sent us your address, so I decided to visit. At first I wasn't sure this was your apartment, because I didn't see the Buick."

Doris set down the bag of groceries she was carrying. "What?" she said again. "The Buick? My friend Alex is keeping it for me. Eleanor, I can't — you're here — A visit? Well, that's *won*derful!"

Doris opened her arms, and Ellie melted into them. She breathed in the scents of toilet water and hair spray and powder, and they masked the fishy odor and the old coffee and Maggie Paxton and Bad Things and slamming and stolen gym suits.

"But — but how did you get here?" asked Doris. "Why didn't you tell me you were coming? Does your father know you're here? You didn't run away, did you?" Before Ellie could answer any of these questions, Doris went on, "Come inside, come inside. You can sit down and tell me everything."

Doris wrestled the door to 3B open and stepped through it with her groceries. Ellie followed, and found herself in a small dim room. It was lit by one window, through which she could see a pipe clinging to a cement wall. At the end of the room was a counter and behind that, a sink and a stove and a graying Amana refrigerator. The rest of the room was crowded by a couch, an armchair, a chest of drawers, a table, and two stools.

"Wow," said Ellie. "This is . . . great. What is it, the living room?"

Doris laughed. "Hon, this is the apartment. The whole thing. Well, except for the bathroom. That's through there." Doris pointed to a doorway off the kitchen.

"This is the entire apartment?" Ellie tried to keep her voice from wobbling or cracking. She knew that Doris was probably still getting established, but she had expected something bigger, especially now that Doris was on Broadway. How on earth were all the Dingmans going to live in this teeny space?

"It's just for now," Doris said, as Ellie looked around. "This is just a starter place." Ellie nodded. "Well, come on, Eleanor. Tell me everything! Tell me how you got here."

Ellie and Doris sat together on the couch, and Ellie leaned into her mother and tried to figure out how to tell her what she had done. Finally she drew in a breath, pulled away from Doris, and said, "Well, I didn't exactly run away, but Dad doesn't know I'm here."

"Eleanor —"

"I just really needed to see you," Ellie rushed on. And she told her mother the story of how she had traveled to New York City by herself.

When Ellie was finished, Doris looked at her watch. "We better call your father," she said. "He must be going crazy by now."

"I know," said Ellie.

"All right. Come on, then. Get your coat. The phone is half a block away, at the corner."

Ellie followed Doris out of the apartment, down the stairs, outside, and to a telephone booth. She knew she should be feeling meek, like Dorothy in Oz on her way to meet the Wizard. But now that Doris had shown up, Ellie was far too excited to feel meek, or even very worried.

"How much change do you need to call Dad?" Ellie asked as they jammed themselves into the booth.

"None. I'll call him collect," Doris replied, and dialed the operator. Ellie stood patiently, waiting for her mother to start explaining things to Mr. Dingman. Instead, Doris suddenly thrust the phone at Ellie and said, "Okay, it's your dad. Tell him where you are."

Surprised, Ellie took the receiver and put it to her ear in time to hear her father say breathlessly, "Hello? Doris?"

"Hi, Dad."

"Ellie? Is that you? I thought your mother was calling. Where are you?"

Ellie paused. "Well, actually, I'm . . . in New York City."

"What? You're where?"

"In New York City. With Doris."

For a moment, Mr. Dingman said nothing. Then he asked quietly, "How did you get there?"

"On a bus. I bought a ticket with my savings."

"After I told you you couldn't go."

Ellie wet her lips. "Yes."

"Did your mother know you were coming?"

"No. I, um, surprised her."

"I see."

"Do you want to talk to her? She's right here," Ellie said helpfully.

"Put her on, please."

Ellie handed the phone back to Doris, and stood first on one foot, then the other as she waited to hear Doris's end of the conversation. Mr. Dingman must have had a lot to say, because for more than a minute, Doris did nothing but listen. Idly, she twirled a lock of hair. She stared out the phone booth. She waved at a man who turned the corner onto the block. Then suddenly she burst out, "I did *not* know she was coming! It was a surprise to me, too. . . . Mm-hmm . . . mm-hmm. . . . Absolutely not. Well, not tonight, anyway. It would be much too late." There was another long pause, and then Doris said, "This is my fault? How is this my fault? Tell me." She put her hand on her hip. "You're the one she ran away from. This doesn't look very good for you, you know."

"I didn't run away!" exclaimed Ellie.

"Well, I know you need her there, but she's *here*," Doris continued. "Look, I don't particularly want —"

Doris broke off abruptly as she glanced down at Ellie. "Why don't you let her stay here for a couple of days," she continued more gently. "It sounds like she could use a break. . . . Albert and Marie? Well, I don't know. I didn't think about that."

Mr. Dingman's voice on the other end of the line was so loud that Ellie clearly heard him say, "You never think!" Doris held the phone away from her ear and mouthed to Ellie, "Thanks a lot."

Ellie, trembling now, said, "Could I talk to him again, please?"

"Be my guest." Doris smacked the receiver into Ellie's outstretched hand.

"Dad?" said Ellie. "I just wanted to tell you that Holly didn't know what I was going to do. She really didn't. So she shouldn't get into trouble. I told her I needed a break for a day. That was all. And Dad? I'm sorry about Albert and Marie. I had them all taken care of for today, but I didn't think about the rest of the week."

Mr. Dingman's sigh floated along the telephone wires with terrible weariness. "There's a problem here, Ellie," he replied. "But you know what? It isn't yours and it isn't you. It's much bigger than you. Don't worry about Albert and Marie. They aren't your responsibility. I'll call the ladies. Maybe they can help out for a couple of days."

"Or maybe Holly can babysit. I'll pay her. I still have a little money left over."

"Like I said, this isn't your responsibility. Let me talk to Doris again, okay?"

"Okay. 'Bye, Dad. I'll see you soon."

Ellie, ashamed, slumped against the side of the phone booth, stared at the sidewalk, and rolled two dimes around in her pocket while she waited for her mother to end the conversation, which she did with an angry "No problem!" and slammed the receiver into the cradle. Then she leaned her forehead against the phone, muttered "Crap," and pounded the receiver into the cradle five more times.

"I'm sorry, Doris, I'm sorry," Ellie said, backing out of the booth.

Doris closed her eyes, opened them, put a smile on her face, and said, "It's okay. Never mind. Listen, I have to make one more call. Why don't you go back to the apartment." She dug in her purse. "Here's the key. You know where to go, right? Make yourself at home. I'll be there in a few minutes."

"Okay." Ellie took the key and walked slowly along the block. Once, she looked over her shoulder at the phone booth, but she couldn't see Doris, who was hidden by a large oak tree.

Ellie trudged up the stairs to 3B and let herself inside.

She flopped on the couch, but almost immediately jumped to her feet again, restless. She walked around and around the room, peering at everything. She didn't see a bed and would have to ask Doris about that. She noted the chest of drawers, which she assumed were filled with Doris's clothes. Spread across the top were Doris's combs and sunglasses and assorted plastic jewelry, tiny bottles of this and that, a can of hair spray, and some coins that did not look like any money Ellie had ever seen. On the table was a stack of movie magazines.

In the kitchen, Ellie peeked in the bag of groceries and saw that it contained a package of paper plates, a box of Kleenex, six cans of Fresca, and a box of saltines. Tacked to the walls of the kitchen were coupons and flyers and eight black-and-white snapshots of Doris with people Ellie had never seen before. Ellie took a look around the rest of the room for photos of her or Marie or Albert or their father, and for the Christmas cards that she and Marie had made and that Mr. Dingman had promised to mail to Doris, but she saw none of these things.

"Doris?" Ellie said the moment she heard the door to the apartment open. "Where —"

Before she could finish speaking, Doris exclaimed, "Fabulous news, Eleanor! Tonight you and I are going to go out to dinner with some of my showbiz friends."

Nothing Like Her

"What?" Ellie stared at Doris. "Tonight? But I just got here."

"Well, I know, hon. But these friends are important to me. Don't you want to meet them?"

"Are they in the Broadway play with you?" Ellie asked tightly.

Doris cleared her throat. "They're ... they're just my good friends. But look, if it really matters to you, I'll call them back and tell them I can't come after all. I just have to run back down to the phone."

"No, don't do that." Ellie slumped sulkily onto the couch. "I don't want you to change your plans."

"Really?" Doris brightened. "Great. I think you'll have fun tonight. I know! We'll get dressed up. Come on. You need to change out of those pants if we're going to go to Café Lune."

Café Lune was a small, very dark restaurant not far from Doris's apartment, with a bar that took up more than half the room. And Doris's friends — there were four of them, two men and two women, none of them married — were crowded into a booth at the back. They greeted Doris heartily and Ellie vaguely. Then they ordered drinks and all began talking at once. Hardly any of them listened to the others. Ellie tried to listen to all of them. As far as she could tell, both of the women had once been showgirls, and one, Jo, was now working as a singing waitress in a large restaurant in Midtown, while the other, Tina, was looking for a job. One of the men, Alex, used to play a character named Todd on a soap opera and now worked in the mailroom of a publishing company, and the other, Paolo, had just auditioned for a revue. "It's at the Centurion Theatre. That's the smallest of the small," he added for Ellie's benefit. "But who cares. It's a job."

While Paolo was talking, Alex was gazing at Ellie and trying to stab an olive in his glass with a toothpick. Suddenly he said, "So you're really Doris's daughter?"

Ellie, who had been feeling sleepy, jerked her head up. "Me?" she said. "Well, yes." She frowned.

"Sorry," Alex said, stabbing at the olive again. "It's just that you look nothing like her."

"And also," said Tina, "she never mentioned you before."

Ellie felt herself shrinking. She truly thought that she was growing smaller. Or that the bench on which she was seated was spreading away from her somehow, swallowing her.

"Oh, now," Doris said with a laugh.

Ellie straightened up. She glared furiously at Doris, then turned back to Tina. "For your information," she said, "Doris also has a son and another daughter." She paused. "And a husband."

"Listen, kid, I'm sorry," said Tina. "Maybe she mentioned you guys. I don't know. Who can remember?"

"Of course I mentioned them!" said Doris gaily.

"Really?" Ellie said sweetly. "Did she also tell you that we all live up in Spectacle, and we're waiting for Doris to start earning enough money so she can move us down here with her?"

Alex's eyes widened. "So you can what?" He hesitated, then said, "Eleanor, really, darling. You don't look anything like your mother. There's almost no resemblance. It's uncanny."

"Yes, the lack of resemblance is uncanny," said Paolo. He smiled to himself, then pulled a small spiral notebook out of his pocket and scribbled something on it with a Bic pen. "That's a good line," he murmured.

"Are we almost done here?" Ellie asked Doris.

"Why, Eleanor, we haven't even ordered yet."

Ellie crossed her arms. "I don't care."

"Eleanor," said Doris. "This behavior strikes me as rude."

Ellie looked at her mother. "That sounds like a line from a play. Are you rehearsing, or is this real life?"

"Eleanor, I'm not kidding. You are asking for it." Doris glanced around the table at Tina and Jo and Paolo and Alex. She tried to laugh. "Don't pay any attention to Eleanor. She's just tired. She had a long day. Come on, let's order dinner. You might as well eat, Eleanor. As soon as you're done we'll go home."

Eleanor Roosevelt Dingman rested her forehead in her hands. She wanted to cry.

Ellie managed not to cry, but only just barely. When the waiter came to their table with his pad and pencil, she ordered a hamburger. Then she sat mutely while the grown-ups talked. Their chatter floated around her and over her and she was largely ignored.

Oh, well, she said to herself, which made her think of Holly. And then for some reason she thought of the cheerful Mouseketeers, in particular of Annette with her dimples and her bright smile. What would Annette do if she were in Ellie's place? She would make the best of it, Ellie decided. She would tell herself that she was in *New York City!* She was eating dinner in a *restaurant* —

late at night! She was with people who were ordering drinks with olives and talking about showbiz. And tomorrow she was probably going to go sightseeing. She would visit Central Park and the Empire State Building. Which reminded Ellie of what she had said in school on Friday. Which further reminded her that New York City was supposed to be her escape from the sparrows, and that if she were truly going to live here one day, she probably shouldn't antagonize Doris.

Ellie ate the last bite of her hamburger, rested her knife carefully on the edge of her plate, folded her hands, and placed them primly in her lap. She tried to smile in a sophisticated way at Jo, who was now telling a story about singing "Happy Birthday" to someone while lying on top of a piano. She didn't utter another word until Doris looked at her watch, heaved a sigh, and said, "Well, I guess Eleanor and I should go. It's getting late." She turned to Ellie. "Ready, hon?"

"I'm ready."

Ellie and Doris said their good-byes and made their way out of the restaurant, Ellie now determined to remain cheerful.

"So how did you meet your friends?" she asked as she and Doris walked through the streets of New York. Considering that it was after eleven o'clock, Ellie was surprised at how busy Seventh Avenue was. At this hour, Witch Tree Lane would be dark and silent, most of its residents already asleep. But here in New York City, Ellie saw people and dogs and cabs and buses, just as she had in the broad light of the afternoon.

"Oh, at auditions mostly," Doris replied. "Now we try to get together a few times a week."

Back in Doris's apartment, Ellie rummaged through her suitcase and found her nightgown and toothbrush. "Hey," she said suddenly. "Doris, where's your bed?"

Doris smiled. "Right here." She removed the cushions from the couch, pulled at a small metal handle, and a bed emerged from within. *"Voilà!"* she exclaimed. "A convertible sofa bed. We can both sleep on it."

Ellie was content to snuggle up to Doris, but had trouble falling asleep. At home in the winter the only nighttime sounds she was aware of were made by Kiss, Marie, and her alarm clock. Here, Ellie heard clinking, pounding, hissing, rumbling, and, briefly, voices so loud that she thought surely they must somehow be in Doris's apartment. But eventually she began to feel drowsy.

"I'm sorry I was rude," she whispered.

"That's okay," Doris whispered back. "It's already forgotten."

* * *

Ellie slept soundly until the morning. The first time she woke up, the clock in the kitchen read 6:52. Ellie watched the light in the single window brighten, watched Doris's chest rise and fall, listened to voices and footsteps in the hallway, curled herself against Doris's back, and fell asleep again.

Doris Has a Secret

At seven-thirty an alarm rang, causing Ellie to jump and Doris to get out of bed with much greater speed than Ellie had expected.

"Morning, hon," said Doris. "Sleep okay?"

"Fine." Ellie sat up in the sofa bed and watched Doris dress in a plain blue skirt and jacket, a white blouse, nylons, and a pair of black pumps. She left all of her jewelry on her dresser, then checked herself in a small mirror mounted near the door to the apartment.

"All right, Eleanor. I'm off to work."

"Aren't you going to eat breakfast before you leave?"

"Oh, I'll grab something on the way." Doris paused. "There isn't really much food in the fridge, but you can get a great breakfast at Ollie's. Just turn left when you leave the building, and Ollie's will be on the corner." Doris opened her purse. "Here," she said, handing Ellie a few bills. "You'll probably want to get lunch there, too. I'll be home around six."

"Six? What am I going to do all day? Can't I come to the theater with you?"

"The theater? . . . Oh! Oh, no." Doris laughed. "No, that wouldn't be a good idea. You'd be bored."

"No, I wouldn't."

"Eleanor, I can't bring you with me. But we can spend the evening together. You're in New York City, for heaven's sake. Go exploring today."

"It's really okay to explore by myself?"

"Sure. Just be careful. Use your head."

"How do I get around?" asked Ellie. "On the subway? I don't even know where the subway is."

Doris considered this. "No, the subway's a little confusing. But you can take a bus, if you can figure out the routes. Or take cabs." She handed Ellie two more bills. "Or walk. That's the most fun. New York is a great city for walking. Just pay attention to the neighborhoods you're in. Do you know anything at all about New York?"

"I've read a little."

"What would you like to see?"

"Central Park and the Empire State Building."

"Well, you can easily walk to Central Park from here. Just go over to Fifth Avenue — you'll want to see Fifth Avenue — and then turn left and walk a couple of blocks and you'll be at one end of the park. Also, you'll be at the Plaza —"

"The Plaza? The Plaza *Hotel*?" squeaked Ellie.

"The Plaza Hotel. Listen, I really do have to get

going," said Doris. "Have fun today. Be careful. I'll see you back here at six, okay? Here's the spare key to the apartment."

"Okay."

Doris hurried away, and Ellie stood by the door for a few minutes, taking stock of her feelings. She was disappointed, and a little hurt, that Doris had left her. She was embarrassed that Doris thought she would be bored spending the day in the theater. She was nervous about being on her own in New York City. But mostly she was excited.

Ellie added the bills that Doris had given her to the remainder of her own money. She totaled it up and was satisfied. Then she found a pen and a pad of paper in Doris's kitchen, sat on the unmade convertible sofa bed, and began writing a plan for the day:

1. Go to Ollie's for breakfast. REMEMBER TO LOCK THE DOOR WHEN YOU LEAVE THE APARTMENT!!!
2. Ask someone at Ollie's how to get to Fifth Avenue.
3. At Fifth Avenue, turn left.
4. Look in the store windows.
5. See if you're allowed in the Plaza Hotel.
6. Walk around Central Park.
7. Eat lunch somewhere — hot dog vendor?

8. Ask someone how to get to the Empire State
   Building OR
   find a bookstore OR
   buy souvenirs for Albert and Marie.
9. Do NOT spend all the money today.
10. Be sure to get home before Doris does.

Ellie read her plan over several times, then got ready
for her breakfast at Ollie's. While she was dressing (she
chose some of her best school clothes), she realized that
she had never eaten breakfast in a restaurant, had never
eaten alone in a restaurant, and had never paid for a
meal by herself. She thought about Thanksgiving dinner at the Starlight and remembered her father allowing
extra tip money for Lorna. Was that something that was
done only on holidays, or was it done every day? Ellie
wished she could ask Doris, but realized she could
watch the other diners at Ollie's and do whatever they
did. She added SEE IF PEOPLE ARE TIPPING!!! To
the end of #1 on her plan.

Then she put on her coat, tucked her plan and the
money in her coat pocket, stepped into the hallway of
the apartment building, locked the door, and dropped the
key down her sock, wiggling her ankle until she felt the
key beneath the arch of her foot. Ellie was ready for her
day in New York City.

When she stepped out of the vestibule, greeted by air much cleaner and fresher than she had expected, Ellie suddenly drew herself up straight and decided that today she, too, would be an actress. She would act as if she had lived in New York City her whole life and knew exactly what she was doing. If this went well it would be a good sign, a sign that she would be able to manage if the Dingmans ever did move to New York City to live with Doris. And so, when she reached the bottom of the crumbling steps, Ellie turned confidently to the left, walked to the corner, and entered Ollie's, which turned out to be a coffee shop not too different from the Starlight Diner.

Ellie sat at the counter, studied the menu the waitress handed her, ordered scrambled eggs, toast, and orange juice, and paid close attention to the man next to her when his bill arrived. She watched him pay for his meal, then slide a quarter underneath his plate before he left. So later, Ellie did the same after she had paid her bill. On her way out of Ollie's she asked the cashier how to get to Fifth Avenue, then (sticking to her plan) she walked to Fifth Avenue and turned left.

Although she once again found herself in a tunnel of towering buildings, she realized that she was already growing used to this sight. She no longer felt the need to stop and stare upward. Now she gawked at what was on the ground — fancy stores with jewels (probably diamonds) right in the windows, ladies nearly as dressed up as Ann Miller in *Easter Parade,* hot dog vendors and hot chestnut vendors and peanut vendors.

Ellie looked at a street sign, realized she should be just about at the Plaza Hotel, turned a corner, and there it was.

"Oh," Ellie said under her breath. It was large and beautiful, carpeted steps leading to the front doors, horse-drawn carriages standing nearby. And across a side street, she saw an expanse of trees, paths, and grassy areas, which surely must be Central Park.

Ellie felt as though she spent the rest of the morning gawking. She gawked inside the Plaza, which she was indeed allowed to enter, gawked as she walked through Central Park, and gawked at vendors until she decided to buy a hot dog from one for lunch. In the afternoon she poked in stores and bought souvenirs for Marie and Albert, then suddenly realized she was exhausted, so she returned to Doris's apartment, which she found without any trouble.

Ellie unlocked the door to 3B, carefully put her purchases in her suitcase, sat on the armchair, and looked at her watch. Three-ten. Doris wouldn't be home for almost three hours. Ellie finished her Nancy Drew book. Three forty-two. Now what? She looked around Doris's apartment for something else to read. She found nothing but the movie magazines. Bored, she decided to see if maybe, just maybe, her mother had squirreled away a photo or two, or the Christmas cards she and Marie had made. She knew she would feel better if she found any little thread connecting Doris to the rest of the Dingmans. So she rummaged through the dresser drawers and then started on the drawers in the kitchen.

In the kitchen drawers were dish towels, some plastic forks and spoons, and a stack of receipts. Ellie examined the receipts. One edge of each was perforated, as if something had been torn off. At the top of each was the word "Gimbel's."

Gimbel's.

Ellie sat down hard on the kitchen floor. *Gimbel's*. These were pay stubs. Doris's name was on each one. Doris's job was not at a theater. It was at a department store.

Ellie, numb, managed to sit through dinner at Ollie's with Doris that night. She said nothing about the pay stubs. The next morning she awoke long before Doris did, dressed and brushed her teeth, then climbed back in bed and pulled the covers around her.

"See you tonight, Eleanor," Doris called as she left the apartment.

"See you."

Ellie was wrapped in a cocoon of covers, but the moment she heard Doris start down the stairs, she leaped out of bed and grabbed her coat. Then she swiped one of the strange-looking coins from the dresser. She had learned that the coins were subway tokens, and had seen Doris drop two of them in her coat pocket every morning before she left the apartment.

Still shrugging into her coat, Ellie locked Doris's door as quickly as she was able. She ran down the stairs. When she reached the vestibule, she burst through it, then stood on the stoop and looked first right, then left. She caught sight of Doris across the street from Ollie's. Ellie sprinted after her and managed to follow her until Doris hurried into a subway station.

Ellie ran in behind her, saw people dropping their tokens into turnstiles, saw Doris already through the turnstile, and saw her step into a subway car just as the doors closed and the train pulled away.

Ellie skidded to a halt. She looked at a map of the subway system, a tangle of confusing lines, felt the token in her pocket, let go of it, and felt for her money. Then, breathing heavily, she left the station and stood at the curb, arm raised.

"Taxi!" she called, and when one drew up next to her, Ellie hopped in and said, "Gimbel's, please. And hurry," just as if she were in a movie.

What Doris Wants

The taxi took Ellie first east, then north. She watched the street numbers rise and rise. As they crossed 79th Street, Ellie said to the driver, "How much farther?"

"Just a few blocks," he replied, and a few minutes later he pulled up in front of a large department store.

Ellie paid the driver, then stood looking into the store. It was much bigger than Harwell's. She stepped inside and walked through the aisles until she saw a store directory. That was no good. She didn't know what department Doris worked in.

Then a thought occurred to her, one she found quite cheering. Maybe Doris was a model here, just as she had been at Harwell's. That wasn't as good (in terms of getting established) as an acting job, but it was better than working as a salesgirl. It was a step in the right direction.

Ellie located the information desk and waited until the woman seated behind it glanced at her.

"Excuse me," said Ellie. "Do you know if there's anyone working here named Doris Dingman?"

"Doris Dingman?"

"How about Doris Day?"

"Oh, sure," said the woman. "She's at the perfume counter." She pointed Ellie in the right direction.

While Ellie was riding in the cab she had rehearsed what she might say to Doris. But now as she approached the perfume counter and caught sight of her mother in her plain blue suit, a bottle of perfume raised in one hand as she offered a customer a sample spray, the words were erased from her mind.

For a moment, Ellie just stared. Then the customer walked away. Ellie stepped closer. "Doris?" she said.

Doris dropped the perfume bottle and it fell to the floor, where it shattered.

Ellie wanted to feel bad for her mother; wanted to be taken in by the look of alarm on Doris's face; wanted to comfort her when she saw tears gathering in her eyes. But all she felt was anger. Doris had lied and cajoled and promised. Doris had betrayed her. Doris had betrayed all the Dingmans.

Ellie's mother was on her hands and knees now, mopping up the perfume with a towel, and brushing the pieces of broken glass into a small heap. "Oh, lord," she muttered. She glanced up and down the aisle, then over her shoulder at a cashier.

Ellie was tempted to help her mother, but she stood

where she was, hands clasped behind her back, eyes fastened on Doris.

"This is your acting job?" she said finally.

"Eleanor —"

"Don't tell me it's just your day job, because I know you don't have a night job. Unless you get paid for sitting around Café Lune with — with —" Ellie found that she couldn't remember the names of the people she'd met on Monday night; found that they were already both nameless and faceless.

"Eleanor!" Doris's tears had vanished. She stood slowly, then brought her fist down on the counter, and Ellie knew she had gone too far.

Ellie turned and saw a woman approaching, a woman who apparently worked at Gimbel's, who was wearing a no-nonsense black suit, with a nameplate on the lapel. "I'd better go," said Ellie. "I think this is your supervisor. And I don't want you to lose this job. Otherwise, how will you be able to afford —" She was going to say, "all those meals at Café Lune," but changed her mind and said, "— to bring the rest of us to New York in June? I'll see you tonight, Doris."

Ellie returned to Doris's apartment and spent a miserable day there. She sat in the dark room, and the sparrows entered her mind and settled there like flies on a car-flattened squirrel. No matter how she tried to chase them away, they returned. The slamming, the ignoring, the humiliating, the teasing, the jeering. New York, moving to Gotham, was supposed to have been Ellie's escape. And she was quite certain now that the Dingmans would not be moving to New York. Not on Doris's salary as a perfume girl at Gimbel's. Maybe her father could find construction work in New York. Ellie tried to picture him living and working in the big city, driving his pickup through the crowded streets and avenues, and was absolutely unable to do so. No. Her father would not leave Spectacle.

The only remotely cheering thought Ellie had on this long, dreary day was that surely Doris would come home to Witch Tree Lane now. Maybe she would even travel back with Ellie. It wouldn't take her long to pack up her things.

Ellie might not be able to escape Spectacle, but Doris could go back to it, and their family would be whole again.

Doris returned promptly at six o'clock. She bustled through the door, saw Ellie sprawled on the rumpled sheets of the sofa bed, and said, "Put on your coat. We're going to Ollie's for dinner."

"Again?" Ellie said without looking at her. "It's cheaper to eat at home."

"That's fine if you want margarine and beer. Otherwise, put on your coat."

Ellie, scowling, put on her coat and followed Doris sullenly into the hallway and down the stairs. When they were seated at a booth in Ollie's, Doris handed Ellie a menu and said, "Order first. Then we'll talk."

Ellie ordered a hamburger and a Coke, then sat back, crossed her arms, and glared at her mother.

Doris glared back, but soon lowered her eyes and reached across the table for Ellie's hand. "Look, Eleanor," she began, "the thing is, I didn't have much luck finding acting jobs here. I tried, I *really did*," she said when she saw Ellie open her mouth. "I had head shots taken as soon as I could. They were very expensive, by the way, but you have to think of them as an investment. I found an agent, too, and I went to auditions. But there's a lot more competition here than there is in Spectacle. Do you know how many people show up at an audition? Sometimes hundreds, depending on the part."

Ellie, listening to Doris, felt a chill on her back and she shivered. She was afraid — her body was telling her to be afraid — but she didn't know why. Something about what Doris was saying, or not saying.

"Well," said Ellie after a moment, "that's too bad. You

must be really disappointed." And then, studying Doris's face, Ellie knew why she was afraid. She was afraid because Doris didn't look one bit disappointed.

"I guess," replied Doris, "but the job at Gimbel's is all right."

Ellie knew what she had to say next, and she felt her breath start to come in little gasps. She put her hands under the table so Doris wouldn't see that they were shaking. "So . . . so you'll be coming back to Spectacle, then, right?" Ellie said in a small voice. She was looking down at the table, at the water glasses, at the salt-and-pepper shakers, but finally she raised her eyes to Doris, and Doris, ever so slowly, shook her head at Ellie.

"You could come back with me," Ellie rushed on. "We can go tomorrow. Or on the weekend if you need more time to get ready. We just have to buy another bus ticket. Albert and Marie would be so happy."

"Eleanor —"

"We all would. We miss you so much. Dad is —"

"Eleanor —"

"Dad's trying really hard."

Ellie wanted to add, "You *have* to come back. You have to help me. Everyone hates Holly and me. They took my clothes in gym, and all the girls saw my bare chest. And they were slamming us. Do you know what that means? They shoved us and hit us and stepped on us. Our clothes were torn, and we were bruised. And we *hurt*. Every part of us hurt, especially our souls."

But Ellie slid her eyes across the table and saw that now Doris couldn't look at her at all.

"Eleanor," Doris said again.

No. I do not want to hear this.

"Eleanor, I'm going to stay in New York," Doris said finally. "This is my new life. I can't — Spectacle — I'm stifled by Spectacle."

"But what do you have here?" whispered Ellie, even though she was fairly certain she knew the answer.

The waitress arrived with their food, and Ellie glanced at her plate, then pushed it away.

"Well," said Doris, "I have . . ." She paused. "I have excitement."

Ellie nodded. She understood perfectly. Doris had a life that seemed glamorous, at least compared to life in Spectacle or Baton. She lived in a city that was nearly as bright at night as it was during the day. And she could spend her evenings with friends in theaters or restaurants or nightclubs, instead of eating supper in front of *The Ed Sullivan Show* and badgering Albert to do his homework. So what if she had to sell perfume during the day? So what if her apartment was the size of a walnut and her refrigerator held only margarine and beer? Gotham was at her feet. And Ellie couldn't compete with it.

Ellie slid out of the booth, pulling her coat after her. "You," she said, pointing her finger at Doris and beginning to sob, "are supposed to be my mother." Her voice rose high enough so that the people in the next booth turned to look at her as she ran through Ollie's and thrust herself out the door and into the night.

Mouse Trap

Ellie ran down the block toward Doris's apartment. It wasn't the first time she'd been outside in the city at night, but it was the first time she'd been in the New York night alone. Everything — doorways and stoops and barred windows — seemed to be crowded together and just inches away from Ellie as she hurried along, her chest heaving.

She reached the stairs to Doris's building, climbed them two at a time, and was about to open the door to the vestibule when she saw a figure slouched in the corner. It was a man, dressed in dark clothes, leaning against the wall and smoking a cigarette. When Ellie saw him she shrieked and drew her hand back as if the door handle had burned her fingers.

The man laughed. Then he took a step toward Ellie and kicked the door open with a boot-clad foot. "Come on in," he said.

Ellie could feel the key to Doris's apartment in her shoe. Even if she dared run by the man and up to the third floor, it would take her forever to get the key out of her sock, and what if he followed her? She looked at the man's grinning face, noticing that he was missing a bottom front tooth, looked at his burning cigarette, ash falling to the floor, looked at his large boots and large hands — and turned around and ran back down the steps. She was sprinting along the sidewalk, listening for the sound of running feet behind her, when she realized she was headed not for Ollie's, but away from it.

Oh, well, she said to herself. If she turned right at the corner, and right at the next corner and then right at the *next* corner she would get to Ollie's from the other direction. But at the very first corner she paused and looked over her shoulder and saw that the man was indeed following her. Panicked, Ellie realized that the stoplight was about to change. If she ran through it, he would be stuck waiting at the corner. So Ellie ran straight ahead, and then turned left because she could make that light, too. And when she looked over her shoulder again, there was the man darting through the cars and trucks against the first light.

Ellie let out another small scream, reached the next corner, saw a stream of traffic before her, and turned right. She was on an unfamiliar block, one that seemed darker and quieter than Doris's. It was so quiet, in fact, that the footsteps Ellie could hear behind her sounded like those of a giant crashing along. Ellie was breathing heavily now and her chest ached, but she increased her speed and pounded to the corner, turned right, and felt a surge of relief when she realized she was on a busy avenue, with cars and people and stores that were still open. She paused outside a greengrocer's, trying to catch her breath, and as she looked in the store window, she saw herself in the reflection and nearly threw up when another figure appeared over her shoulder. The figure was dark, and Ellie could see the glow from the tip of a cigarette. Certain she was about to feel hands grab her shoulders, she darted off, ran to the corner, saw that once again she had reached a light that was about to change, and hurtled through the intersection. She was too terrified to look over her shoulder, so she kept running. She ran through lights, and turned right and left and right and left again until she had absolutely no idea where she was. The street signs told her she was at the corner of Broadway and 45th. So she was south of Doris's apartment, but where was Broadway? She couldn't remember.

Ellie found herself in a crowd of people. Feeling safer, she glanced around. She couldn't see the man. No one lurking and looming in dark clothes and big boots. Ellie stopped outside a small store that sold newspapers and magazines and cigarettes and candy. The name of the store was painted gaily on an awning over the front door: FUNNY CRY HAPPY. Ellie frowned. Then she glanced around once more and entered the store.

"Excuse me," she said to a man seated behind the counter. "Do you have a telephone I could use?"

"Telephone? Telephone?" the man repeated shrilly. He spoke with a thick accent. "You want telephone? Use pay phone on street. You customer? You buy something? Even if you customer you use pay phone on street."

"But," said Ellie, her voice catching, "you don't understand. Someone's after me. Someone's been following me. A man. I can't go back out there."

"What? What?"

"I need to use the phone. It's an emergency!" Ellie cried.

"Emergency? What is emergency?"

"I just told you. Someone's after me. I have to call my —" Ellie suddenly realized she couldn't call Doris. Doris didn't have a phone. "I — I have — I have —" Ellie burst into tears.

"You wait. You in trouble? You wait here," said the man. "I get Marta. Marta talks to you. Okay? You wait I get Marta."

"Don't leave me!" called Ellie, but the man had already rushed out from behind the counter and disappeared through a door at the back of the store.

"Marta?" Ellie could hear him call. This was followed

by an explosion of foreign words, and then a woman about Doris's age hurried through the door and along an aisle until she reached Ellie.

"Hello?" she said. "Is anything wrong?"

"Yes," said Ellie, and she tried to explain about the man, but her words came out so fast and were so blurred by her sobs that the woman finally placed her hands on Ellie's shoulders, guided her to a stool behind the counter, and sat her on it.

"Hang on just a minute, okay?" said Marta. She disappeared through the door at the back of the store, then returned with a glass of water, which she handed to Ellie.

Ellie gulped it, then blurted out, "I'm being followed!"

"You're being followed? Who's following you?"

"A man."

Marta's eyes widened. "Are you sure?"

"Well, I *was* being followed." Ellie's pounding heart began to slow down. She glanced outside.

Marta glanced outside, too, then looked at her watch. "Maybe I'll just close up the store," she said. She flipped over a sign hanging on the front door so that the OPEN side was facing in, then cupped her hands and peered through the window. "No one's out there now," she said.

Ellie slumped on the stool. "I've been running for a long time. I guess I lost him somewhere."

"Who was this man?" asked Marta.

Ellie shrugged. "I don't know." She told Marta what had happened, leaving out her fight with Doris.

"Well, let's call your mom," said Marta.

Ellie looked down at the countertop. "I can't. She doesn't have a phone."

"Well, then, I think," Marta said gently, "that we ought to call the police."

"The police?" Ellie squeaked. "No, no. I'll just call my dad, okay? Um, how do you make a long-distance telephone call?"

Marta, looking suspicious, pulled a phone out from under the counter, and dialed it for Ellie. "Here you go," she said, handing her the receiver.

"Hello?" Ellie heard her father say.

"Dad, it's me." Ellie burst into tears.

It took a long time for Ellie to tell Mr. Dingman what had happened. He listened quietly, and when she was finished, he said, "I'll be right there."

"Right *here?*" said Ellie. "You mean New York City? You're coming to New York City?"

"I'll be there as fast as I can."

"But what about Albert and Marie?"

"I'll figure something out," said Mr. Dingman. "Don't worry. Now can I talk to — What's the name of that woman who's there in the store with you?"

"Marta," said Ellie. "Okay, here she is." Ellie gave the

phone back to Marta, slid off the stool, and walked down one of the aisles in the store. She had the feeling that something unstoppable had just been set in motion. She was the marble in Holly's game of Mouse Trap, and someone (her father or Doris or the man in the vestibule) had turned the little crank, and now Ellie the marble had no choice but to roll along the chutes until she was trapped under the plastic mouse cage.

Ellie heard Marta hang up the phone. "Ellie?" she said. "I'm going to call the police now. Your father won't be here for several hours, and we need to get you home."

"Couldn't you just walk me home?" Ellie asked feebly.

"Honey, the police need to know what happened. You can tell them your story, and they'll take you home."

Ellie nodded.

An hour later, Ellie was sitting on the convertible sofa bed in Doris's apartment. Doris and two policemen were talking at the door.

"I can assure you she's quite safe now," Doris was saying, her hands fluttering by her chest. "I'm sorry you had to bring her home." She flashed a smile at the officers.

The officers did not return the smile. "A child her age shouldn't be out alone," said one.

"Really, it won't happen again," said Doris. "She's only visiting here, anyway."

"We understand the father is on the way," said the other officer.

"Oh, really?" Doris glanced at Ellie.

Ellie couldn't speak. The marble was just rolling along.

One of the officers crossed the room and sat next to Ellie. "You did talk to your father, didn't you?" he said.

"Yes."

"And he's on his way?"

Ellie nodded.

"When do you think he'll be getting here?" Doris asked sharply from the doorway.

"I don't know," said Ellie. "As soon as he can. I guess maybe in a few hours."

The officer looked thoughtful. He reached into his pocket, withdrew a pencil and a small pad, and scribbled something on the top sheet of paper. "Here," he said to Ellie, tearing off the paper. "This is my phone number. You can call me at any time."

Doris gave a small laugh. "We don't have a phone, remember? That's how all this trouble got started."

"Ma'am, you are treading on very thin ice," was all the officer replied. He rested his hand on Ellie's arm. "Are you sure you're okay?"

"Yes," said Ellie.

"All right." The officers took one last look around the apartment and left.

"Eleanor," said Doris, "hon —"

"Shut up," replied Ellie. "I'm not talking to you. You are not my mother."

Mr. Dingman arrived shortly after 3:00 that morning. Doris opened the door for him, and for a moment he simply glared at her. Then he crossed the room and enveloped Ellie in a huge hug.

Ellie, who had fallen asleep on the sofa bed, burrowed against his shirt and willed herself not to start crying again. "How did you get here?" she whispered.

"I drove."

"You *drove?* In the *truck?*"

"Yes," Mr. Dingman said wearily.

"Where are Albert and Marie?"

"At home. The ladies came over. They'll stay with them until we get back."

Ellie nodded.

Mr. Dingman turned to Doris.

"Don't start," Doris said, before Mr. Dingman had said a word.

"'Don't start'?! Our daughter is chased through the streets by some maniac and can't even call you —"

"I *said* don't start."

"Doris, for God's sake — All right, Ellie, get your things together. We're going home."

"Now?" cried Ellie. "Dad, you just drove all night. You can't turn around and leave now. We should leave in the morning. When it's light. And after you've slept for a little while."

Mr. Dingman turned and looked at Doris. "Can we talk for just a moment. Please?"

The conversation was quick and quiet. It took place in the bathroom. When it was over, Doris sat on the sofa bed and said to Ellie, "You and your dad are going to stay here tonight, but I think it's better if I don't stay with you. You have a key, so you can let yourselves out in the morning. Just leave the key under the doormat outside 3A, okay?"

"But Doris, where are you going?" asked Ellie. The marble was approaching the mouse trap.

"I'll go stay with Jo or someone. Don't worry." Doris smoothed Ellie's hair back from her face. "I'm sorry your trip had to end this way," she said. "Eleanor, you know I —"

Ellie sat up. "Don't say it. Don't say anything. Just leave."

Doris stood up and walked out of the apartment.

And the mouse trap fell down around Ellie.

PART FOUR

June

On a warm afternoon in June, Eleanor Roosevelt Dingman sat on her front stoop, Kiss beside her, and let her gaze wander up Witch Tree Lane. She looked for a long time, and she was satisfied.

"It's good, Kiss," she said. "Everything's good."

Kiss bounded down the steps, no longer tethered by a leash. She was probably going to visit the ladies, Ellie thought. Lately, now that the weather had turned warm, Miss Woods and Miss Nelson had begun taking their late afternoon tea on the front porch. If Kiss showed up for this, she was bound to be served a cookie or part of a sardine sandwich.

Ellie's gaze traveled across the street to the Majors' house. Sitting up very straight on the stoop was Smudge, the black-and-white cat Holly had adopted from the animal shelter in April. Ellie watched Smudge give himself a bath, wetting his front paws and rubbing them over and over his ears and face. When he was done bathing, he squatted on his haunches and regarded Ellie gravely.

"Hi, Smudgie," Ellie called. She smiled. Noticeably

absent from the Majors' driveway was Mick's car. It hadn't been parked there in over a month. Ellie didn't like the way Mick had left, but she was glad he was gone.

Ellie watched Kiss's progress down Witch Tree Lane. She passed the Levins' and the Lauchaires' houses. In the Levins' garage, Ellie knew, was a wood frame containing a large pane of glass. "We might as well be prepared for the next broken window," Mr. Levin had said. But no windows had been broken since February. At the end of the Lauchaires' driveway was a brand-new mailbox, painted white with a vine of jaunty strawberries — a present from Monsieur Lauchaire to his wife, not because their old mailbox had been damaged, but just because. Ellie was considering painting the Dingmans' mailbox herself.

Kiss arrived at the ladies' house as their front door opened and Miss Nelson emerged carrying the tray of tea things. Ellie waved to her. From all the way down the street she could see Kiss's tail pick up speed as she sniffed the air, catching the scents of sardines and raisins and other tasty tea fare. (Not that Kiss would turn down much of anything. Ellie had watched her find and eat a dead moth the day before.)

As far as Ellie was concerned the most satisfying sight on the entire street was the ladies' unobstructed front lawn — no FOR SALE sign. They had taken it down in April, shortly after Holly had brought Smudge home.

"We never really wanted to leave, anyway," Miss Woods had said.

And now there didn't seem to be a reason to leave. No Bad Things for four months. Around the Witch Tree, which showed only the faintest traces of purple paint, Miss Nelson had created a garden. Impatiens were blooming among spindly pachysandra plants. "I'll put some bulbs in this fall," she had told Ellie. "Tulips and daffodils and narcissus. Things that will grow taller than the pachysandra." Ellie had mostly been glad that the ladies still expected to be living in their house in the fall — next spring, too, if they wanted to see the new flowers.

Ellie was just wondering if it would be all right to invite herself to tea with the ladies when, across the street, the Majors' front door opened and Holly stepped outside. She bent down to pat Smudge, then saw Ellie, waved to her, and called, "Come over!"

The Majors' front stoop was as tidy as the inside of their house, neatly swept, the old braided mat placed squarely in front of the door.

"Where are Albert and Marie?" Holly asked as Ellie sat down, Smudge between them.

"Mrs. Lauchaire took them into town with Domi and Etienne. They're all getting new sneakers. Dad gave Albert money this morning."

"I wish I could get new sneakers," Holly said glumly. She regarded her faded Keds.

"They don't look so bad," said Ellie.

"No. It's the — what do you call it? The principle of the thing?"

"Because of Mick?"

"Yeah."

Ellie shook her head. "Is your mother still mad?"

"Are you kidding? She'll be mad for months. Maybe years. He got a hundred dollars. A *hundred* dollars! Do you know how long Mom had been saving to get that much? All year, practically."

"Well, at least he's gone."

Mick had left in the middle of the night, after an argument of epic proportions. (Ellie could hear him and Holly's mother all the way across the street, right through her closed window.) On his way out he had swiped Selena's stash of emergency money, which was more for treats and extras than actual emergencies, but still . . .

"I know. But . . . I wouldn't mind new sneakers. These are getting pinchy. My toe is about to break through." Holly wiggled her left big toe. "Oh, well," she said.

Ellie patted Smudge absentmindedly. She closed her eyes and tilted her face upward, feeling the sun on it. She could almost fall asleep, she thought, sitting there in the afternoon warmth, patting Smudge's head, hypnotized.

"So do you think it will last?" asked Holly.

"What?"

"You know."

Ellie sighed. The sparrows. Not much had changed. Ever since Ellie had returned from New York City, bitterly regretting what she had said to Tammy before she'd left, the sparrows had continued to ignore her and Holly. But that was it. No slamming. No more incidents in the locker room. She and Holly had simply resumed their Casper-like existence.

"I guess," said Ellie. "It's not so bad, is it?"

Holly shrugged. She poked at her toe through the canvas. "Could be worse."

Ellie glanced at her watch. "I should probably go," she said. "Marie and Albert will be back soon. Dad, too."

Holly looked at the watch herself. "Gosh, your dad really does get home early now, doesn't he?"

"Five-fifteen exactly, every single afternoon," replied Ellie. "He told his boss he has to be home by then."

"*He* told his *boss* that?"

"Yup. He said it was a condition. He said he could

only take the job if they met all his conditions. And they did. They really wanted him."

"Does he like the job?"

"So far. He says there's nothing like being your own boss, but that this job is better pay and better hours. He's been home every single evening and every single weekend since he started. Albert can't believe it. Even Doris wasn't home this much, and she didn't have a job." Ellie stood and dusted her hands on her pants. "See you tomorrow," she said. "Just think, only two more weeks of school."

"And then seventy-four days of summer vacation," Holly replied blissfully. "I counted on the calendar last night."

Ellie whistled for Kiss, who came bounding off the ladies' porch and rocketed down the street to meet her. Ellie stooped to give her a hug and got a whiff of sardines. "Come on, you little beggar," she said. "Let's go start dinner."

Ellie busied herself in the Dingmans' kitchen, which she had cleaned out, rearranged, reorganized, and decorated. Taped to the refrigerator were a composition Albert had written entitled "My Best Dog," and a Mother's Day card Marie had made in school and presented to Ellie three Sundays earlier. Marie had said nothing about Doris when she gave it to Ellie, only, "I made this for you. It says 'Dear Mom' because that's what Miss Riddel told us to put on the front. But it's really for you."

Ellie set the table, fed Kiss (whose appetite had not been diminished by the sardine sandwich), and washed lettuce for a salad. She was debating whether to defrost some hamburger patties when she looked at her watch and exclaimed, "Five forty-five! Where is everybody? Nobody's home yet, Kiss."

And at that moment the door burst open and in came Mr. Dingman, Albert, and Marie, lugging bags of groceries.

"Sorry we're late," said Mr. Dingman.

"Mrs. Lauchaire was driving by the A&P," said Marie, "and we saw Daddy's truck outside, so she let us out and we got to go grocery shopping with Daddy."

"He wouldn't let us get anything good," Albert said, but Ellie noted that he seemed quite cheerful about this.

Mr. Dingman began unpacking the bags. Onions, potatoes, celery, more lettuce, more hamburger meat, a package of hot dogs, cantaloupes, apples, nectarines, two boxes of cereal, three boxes of macaroni, milk, ginger ale. . . .

Ellie was trying to put everything away in her carefully organized kitchen when her father handed her a paperback book. "Look what I found at the check-out counter," he said.

Ellie read the title aloud. *"Quick Fixes: Healthy Meals in Less Than Thirty Minutes."*

"If you can make the meals in half an hour, they must be pretty simple," said her father. "So I figured even I could make them."

"You?" said Ellie and Marie.

"You're going to cook?" said Albert.

"Why not? I'm home early enough now. Ellie shouldn't have to do all the cooking." He opened the book. "'Simple Summer Fare,'" he read. "Okay. This is what we're going to have tonight. Some kind of simple summer fare. While I'm cooking, the three of you go start your homework. No arguments," he added, glancing at Albert. "If you finish your homework before supper, you can play outside for fifteen minutes before you take your baths."

Mr. Dingman's dinner was a success. When he served it, Albert looked at him with the same kind of respect he usually reserved for Roy Rogers or Superman. And Ellie, feeling just the teeniest pang of jealousy, recovered quickly when she realized that, with her homework done, she could visit with Holly again.

That night, as Ellie lay in bed, the window open, sweet air curling around her and twilight sleep beginning to overtake her, Marie called out, and Ellie jumped. "What is it?" she said, startled.

"My tummy hurts."

"Really? Do you feel like you have to throw up?"

"No. It just hurts. Can I get in bed with you?"

"Sure." Ellie pulled back her covers, and Marie crawled in beside her.

"Ellie? Why haven't we heard from Doris?"

Ellie's eyes opened all the way, but she said evenly, "Oh, you know Doris. She's so busy."

"But when are we going to go live with her? School's almost over. She said we would finish out the school year, then move to New York City."

"I guess we'll have to talk to Dad."

"I miss Doris," Marie said sleepily as she nestled against Ellie.

"I know."

What Comes Your Way

Marie spent the rest of the night curled into Ellie like a kitten, and Kiss never left the bed. In the morning, Marie didn't mention Doris to Ellie, so Ellie didn't mention Doris to their father. The Dingman children went to school, they came home from school, time slipped by, and suddenly it was the next to the last day of the term.

It was on this day that two things took place that reminded Ellie it was impossible, absolutely impossible, to guess what might come your way. The first thing happened just before lunchtime. The bell had rung, and Ellie and her classmates had lined up and filed out of Room 12. Holly had been sent ahead on an errand to the office and was to meet Ellie in the cafeteria. Ellie was hurrying through the hall, feeling the coins she had slipped into her sock that morning along with her key, pleased that she had enough money to buy ice cream for both herself and Holly, when a body slammed into her from behind, sending her toward the wall of lockers. Ellie caught herself, pulling up short, and was slammed again, this time with more force. She hit the lockers with a crash, and even before she touched her hand to her mouth, before she tasted blood and spat a shower of red onto locker #89, she knew that she had split her lip.

Ellie gasped. The attack was unexpected. She had truly thought the slamming had stopped, her ghostly existence firmly in place, a fact of life she was willing to tolerate.

Ellie heard a derisive snort behind her and turned around slowly. She lowered her bloody hand and faced Maggie Paxton. "Nice —" Maggie said, and without thinking, without a single moment of thought, Ellie lunged forward, arms outstretched, and shoved and shoved; shoved Maggie until she banged against the lockers on the other side of the hall and then crumpled to the floor.

Maggie landed with a small cry, but the hall was emptying already, and the few kids who saw what happened didn't know Maggie and Ellie, and they hurried on to the cafeteria or the library or the gym.

Ellie barely noticed them, anyway. She glanced at Maggie, then stepped over her legs and walked down the hall toward the entrance to Washington Irving Elementary. When she reached the door, she walked outside, walked across the schoolyard, and turned right. She had walked nearly half a mile before she began to think about what had happened, and she felt shaky and had to sit down by the side of the road.

She was at the intersection of Route 27 and King Street, cars and trucks whizzing by her, whipping her hair across her face and stinging her eyes. Ellie scooted back from the road. She found a Kleenex in her pocket and she held it to her puffy lip, blotting it until the stains grew smaller. Tentatively she touched her lip with her forefinger. The pain made her gasp, and she pulled her hand away quickly. Then she drew her knees up to her chest, folded her arms across them, and laid her head on her arms.

She had pushed one of the sparrows. She had humiliated her, and left her on the floor. She had done to Maggie what the sparrows had been doing to her and Holly for months, so her behavior was as cruel as theirs. Ellie touched her lip again and realized that, to her surprise, she felt glad she had hurt Maggie. Furthermore, she had no doubt that Maggie, unlike Ellie and Holly, would tell Mr. Pierce what had happened. And then Ellie would get to tell her own story, and everything would be out in the open at last. And with only one more day of school to go — who cared?

Still, Ellie had walked out of school, just left. All her things were in her desk, Holly was waiting for her in the cafeteria, Mr. Pierce would have no idea where she was. She could go back; she could just turn around and go back now and face Maggie and Mr. Pierce and whatever would come her way. Instead, Eleanor Roosevelt Dingman got to her feet and began to walk to Witch Tree Lane.

It was a long walk; a long walk, and the day was very hot. Ellie's hair stuck damply to the back of her neck, and her lip throbbed. She wished for a hat. She wished for a drink of water. She wished for cool hands tending her lip, a voice telling her to lie still, that everything would be all right.

The ladies would be home, thought Ellie as she scuffed through the dust along Route 27. A dump truck barreled by her, showering her with gravel and blaring its horn. Ellie would tell the ladies everything; everything, from the beginning. The ladies would know what to do.

It was when, more than an hour later, Ellie finally turned off of Route 27 and onto Witch Tree Lane that the second unexpected thing happened. She was looking down the lane to see if Millie, the blue truck, was in the ladies' driveway, when she noticed a car in her own driveway.

It was the Buick, and Doris was sitting on the Dingmans' front stoop.

For a moment Ellie stood still and stared. Surely she was seeing things. Maybe she had hit her head when she fell. She shook her head gently, conscious of her lip. She blinked her eyes. The Buick remained in the driveway, and Doris remained on the stoop.

"Doris?" she called.

Doris raised her head and saw Ellie. "Eleanor? What —"

Ellie crossed the front lawn, her hand to her lip.

"Good lord, Eleanor, what *happened* to you?" exclaimed Doris. "What's wrong with your lip?"

Ellie answered with questions of her own. "What are you *doing* here? Why didn't you tell us you were coming back?"

"We better get you inside and fix you up."

Ellie slumped onto the top step, suddenly afraid she might faint. "Okay."

Doris hesitated. "I forgot my key," she said.

Ellie looked up sharply, her head clearing. "You came back and you didn't bring your key?"

"Let's talk about this later. Right now we need to fix your lip. What happened, anyway?" She reached her hand down to Ellie, and Ellie jerked away.

"My lip's fine. Why don't you have your key?"

"I don't want to have a big argument right now,

Eleanor. I think it would be better if I spoke to your father. Where is he working today?"

Ellie stared at her mother. "Don't you know?"

"How would I know where he's working? He works all over the place."

"Not anymore. Not since he got his new job. You do know about Dad's new job, don't you?"

"No . . . what's his job?"

Ellie looked at the Buick in the driveway. She looked at Doris sitting awkwardly on the stoop, encased in a too-tight yellow skirt and a glowing pink jacket, the brightest spot on Witch Tree Lane; a jigsaw piece tossed into the wrong puzzle box.

"Eleanor? What's his job?"

"How could he not have told you about his job?"

"Well —"

"When was the last time you and Dad were in touch?"

"Let's at least put some ice on your lip; then we can talk."

Ellie let out a loud, annoyed sigh, retrieved her house key from her sock, and opened the front door, allowing Doris to pass inside ahead of her. She watched for the signs of someone returning to a well-loved place, a missed place — but saw only a look of agitation as

Doris glanced around Ellie's reorganized kitchen. And another look of agitation as Kiss scrambled down the stairs and flung herself at Ellie, then saw Doris and barked frantically at her before recognition set in.

"What happened to the dish cloths?" Doris asked, peering into the Messy Corner and ignoring Kiss's attempts to lick her hands.

Ellie pointed to a drawer. "They're in there. But don't use a dish cloth. I'll get blood on it." She reached for a paper towel. Then she took two ice cubes from the freezer, wrapped them in the towel, and held the towel to her mouth. "Okay. I have ice on my lip," she said and glared at Doris.

Doris sighed. "Let's sit down. But not in here. It's too hot."

Ellie and Doris returned to the front stoop, preceded by Kiss. "So," said Ellie, staring straight ahead at Holly's house, "when was the last time you spoke to Dad?"

"We haven't actually spoken since you left New York."

"Huh. Very interesting."

"Eleanor —"

"Doris, look. You came here without your key, so I know you aren't moving back. And I know we're not going to be moving to New York City with you. I guess I even know you and Dad are probably going to get divorced now." Kiss dropped down next to Ellie, hindquarters on one step, front feet on the step below, and leaned into her side. "But," Ellie said, and she lowered her voice, humiliated by the prospect of asking this question, more humiliated by why she needed to ask it, "could I maybe go back to New York City with you for a little while? I need to get out of here, too." Ellie watched Doris, willing the answer to be no, but wishing to hear a yes slip from her mother's lips.

Doris turned away and looked down Witch Tree Lane. She rested her hand on Ellie's knee, and Ellie began to tremble.

"Eleanor, the thing is — this is why I came today — well, the thing is that it's time for me to move on. I really would like to give my career one more chance, so I've decided to go to Hollywood." Doris turned to face Ellie with a half smile. "Hollywood," she repeated, as if the word itself implied success.

Ellie jumped to her feet. "WHAT?" Why couldn't Doris just say yes or no like a normal mother? "What?" she cried again. She recalled the moment in the little store in New York City when she had felt herself rolling toward the mouse trap. And quickly, so quickly that the thought buzzed through her mind almost without her being aware of it, she realized that what Doris had just said was going to change Ellie's life again — but this time Ellie was not aware of a mouse cage about to fall around her. She felt Kiss's weight against her side, saw Smudge lolling on his back in the sunshine, smelled cut grass from the Levins' lawn, and she pictured herself, the marble, rolling on toward whatever lay ahead, bravely passing the mouse trap.

Ellie sat down again, this time a foot away from Doris, and Doris glanced at her, then said, "Well, I know it's a shock, but . . ." She looked over her shoulder at the Dingmans' front door, "anyway, I guess I'll be needing some warm-weather things."

"You mean the *rest* of your things," said Ellie. "You mean you came back to get the *rest* of your things."

"Don't be snide, Eleanor. It's a different climate out there. Look, I have to do what I have to do."

"You don't have to do this."

"Yes, I do."

Ellie closed her eyes and formed a picture in her mind: Doris in a red convertible cruising down a wide street lined with palm trees. Her hair is held in place by a red-and-white-polka-dotted kerchief; large red-framed sunglasses are on her nose. She's smiling, she's color coordinated, she works at the checkout counter at the grocery store or the window of the drive-in or as a temporary secretary somewhere, anywhere.

This picture was very detailed, but it didn't tell Ellie whether Doris was happy.

"Doris," said Ellie, "are you happy in New York?"

"Well," Doris said, after a pause. "I guess I was, at first. It's such a glamorous place. But I didn't really get where I wanted to be."

Ellie nodded. She didn't think Doris would get where she wanted to be in Hollywood, either, that she would stay there until the excitement ran out and she began to dream of somewhere else, and then she would move on — to Chicago or Nashville or maybe Mexico or an island. More places without Ellie in them, because the Dingmans weren't enough to make Doris happy, and because Doris could never be happy for very long anyway.

"I see," said Ellie. She hugged Kiss to her for a moment, then stood and opened the screen door, newly patched by Albert. "Okay. I'll go call Dad for you."

Ellie was halfway to the kitchen before she was struck by a thought, and she turned around and stood at the screen door again. "Hey, Doris," she said. "How come you came back in the middle of a weekday? Was it because you knew Albert and Marie and I would be in school? Was it so you wouldn't have to see us?"

Doris tried to laugh, then said, "Oh, for heaven's sake, Eleanor. You know I don't like good-byes."

The Gaze of the Witch Tree

Ellie called her father, and Mr. Dingman, incredulous, said he'd come home as fast as he could.

"You might as well start packing now," Ellie said to Doris. "It'll take Dad a little while to get here."

Doris retrieved two empty suitcases from the Buick and brought them inside, but she didn't start packing. Instead, she toured slowly through the Dingmans' small house — the living room, the dining room, and the kitchen on the first floor, the three bedrooms on the second floor. Ellie trailed after her, trying to see things through Doris's eyes. The house was tidy, and if not exactly sparkling clean like in TV commercials, certainly cleaner than it used to be. Just the weekend before, Mr. Dingman had drawn up a list of chores that must be accomplished every week. He had posted the list on a bulletin board in the kitchen, along with a chart showing which of the four Dingmans was responsible for each chore. Most of the current week's chores had been checked off, and so the vacuuming and dusting had been taken care of, the bathroom floors had been mopped, and the laundry had been started.

Doris paused at the refrigerator and flicked the Mother's Day card open with one polished fingernail. "Marie made a card for me?" she said, smiling at Ellie.

"Nope," Ellie replied. "She made it for me."

"Oh." Doris closed the card, and Ellie felt secretly gratified by the look of dismay on Doris's face.

Upstairs, Doris peered into the bedrooms, saw each bed smoothly made, but said only, "Kiss had a bath, didn't she?"

"On Sunday," replied Ellie.

Doris entered the bedroom she had shared with Ellie's father. There were her things on her bureau, moved slightly since Ellie had recently dusted under them. There was the picture in the tortoiseshell frame of the Dingmans on their wedding day. There was the vial containing baby teeth lost by Ellie, Albert, and Marie. There was the first Christmas present Ellie had bought Doris with her own money — a large blue plastic orchid, meant to be worn as a pin, which Doris had worn once, then had used as a "bureau decoration."

Doris stood by the bed for a moment, then looked out the window. "There's your father," she said.

Ellie watched Doris hurry out of the room, heard her

run down the stairs and meet Mr. Dingman at the front door — a brief greeting and a muffled exchange of words before they disappeared into the kitchen. Ellie tiptoed to the top step of the stairs, sat on it, then silently slid down several more steps, as close to the kitchen as she dared creep.

"Hollywood?" was the first thing she heard her father say. "*Holly*wood?"

"I'm not getting anywhere in New York," replied Doris.

"So come —"

"And you know I can't come back here."

"You can't even say 'home,' can you? You can't even call this place your home."

"I haven't found my home."

Ellie leaned forward, straining, but couldn't make out any words for a while. Then she heard, "All right, I'll call a lawyer. I'd like to get divorced as quickly as possible," and realized it was her father speaking.

Another pause.

"What do you plan to tell the children?" Mr. Dingman asked. Doris's answer was nearly inaudible, but Ellie clearly heard her father say, "Not even that? So it's up to me? Everything's up to me?"

"No, it isn't —"

"That's why you came home when you knew the children would be at school."

"Well..."

"This is great, Doris. It's just great." Mr. Dingman paused. "What *is* Ellie doing at home?" he suddenly thought to ask. "Ellie? Ellie?"

"I better go pack," said Doris.

"Fine. Ellie?"

Ellie and Doris passed quietly on the stairs. Ellie found her father seated at the kitchen table and was about to sit in the chair opposite him when the phone rang. Mr. Dingman reached for it. "Hello?" he said. Then, *"Oh."* He glanced at Ellie. "Yes, she's here.... I don't know. I just got home. I haven't spoken to her.... No, she's fine. Well," (another glance at Ellie) "actually she looks like ... like someone took a swing at her.... What? ... Oh, really? Holly said that? ... I don't know. I'll have to talk to her. And this isn't — I can't — right now is not —" Finally Mr. Dingman looked at his watch. "Would it be possible for me to call you tonight, Mr. Pierce? I'll talk to Ellie this afternoon.... Okay.... Okay, thank you. Good-bye."

Mr. Dingman hung up the phone. "Honey," he said, "what's going on? Holly told Mr. Pierce something —" He stopped speaking and looked closely at Ellie, then pulled her to him, sat her in his lap as if she were three years old again. "Are you really okay?"

Ellie nodded, tears dripping down her nose and making tiny navy spots on her father's blue shirt.

"Your mother is leaving. For good. I guess you know that."

"Yeah. I know about the divorce, too. I was listening," she confessed. "But, anyway, I had already figured it out." Ellie reached for a box of Kleenex, blew her nose, then looked at her watch. "Doris had better hurry. Albert and Marie will be home in an hour and a half."

Mr. Dingman reached for the Kleenex, blew his own nose, then turned Ellie around so she was facing him. "We're going to be all right, you know," he said.

"I know," said Ellie.

"We'd better do something about that lip." Mr. Dingman made a paper-towel compress for Ellie and held it to her mouth. "Does this hurt?"

"Not so much. It's starting to feel better."

Mr. Dingman nodded. "You can tell me what happened later, okay?"

"Okay."

Ellie sat in the kitchen with Kiss, just sat, while her father talked to Doris in the bedroom. Later, after Mr. Dingman had come grimly down the stairs, Ellie went to her parents' room. The suitcases lay open on the bed, overflowing with the contents of Doris's drawers and her closet. Doris stood in the bathroom, clearing small bottles and tubes out of the medicine chest and sweeping them into a makeup case.

"Doris?" said Ellie.

Doris turned around, and Ellie could see the back of her beehive in the mirror. "Yeah?"

"How come I don't call you 'Mom'?"

Doris flashed Ellie a crooked smile. "Well, I wouldn't let you. I made you call me Doris starting when you were a baby."

"I know, but why?"

"I suppose because I never felt like a —"

Ellie glared at her mother.

"'Mom' is so old-fashioned," said Doris.

"Uh-huh." Ellie looked at Doris's bureau. It was a mess, strewn with old bobby pins and rubber bands, things Doris was going to throw away. The wedding photo lay facedown, and the vial of baby teeth and the plastic orchid had been moved to one side.

Ellie sank into the armchair and watched Doris flit from the sink to the bureau to the closet to the suitcases. Doris's presence was huge, as if she were an inflating balloon, taking up all the air and space. There was no room for Ellie. So Ellie crossed the hall and lay on her bed. She slid effortlessly into her private place and was aware only of the leaves on the maple tree outside her window until she heard Doris call, "Eleanor? I'm leaving now."

Ellie got to her feet and looked into her parents' room. Doris was standing by the bed, the packed suitcases at her feet. The plastic orchid was still on the bureau, but the photo and the vial of teeth were gone.

"You've been leaving forever," Ellie replied.

Doris, who had just picked up a suitcase in each hand, lost her grip on them and they thumped to the floor. "I'm sorry," she said. Then she struggled down the hallway with the suitcases.

Ellie watched her for a moment, grabbed the orchid from the bureau, and slipped it into the back of the tote bag that was slung over Doris's shoulder. Then she lay down in the room that was now Mr. Dingman's, and stayed there until at last she heard the Buick pull out of the driveway.

Downstairs, Ellie found her father sitting at the kitchen table, talking on the phone and writing something on a pad of paper. He glanced up at Ellie, then said into the phone, "Excuse me, could you hold for just a moment?"

"I'll meet you on the porch," Ellie mouthed to him, and took Kiss with her to the front stoop.

Ellie sat on the top step once again, grateful for the

shade that was creeping across the front of the house. Kiss plopped down next to her, this time with her head in Ellie's lap. Ellie let out a loud sigh. She stroked Kiss's ears, then leaned back on her elbows and took in the entire street — Holly's neat house; the Levins', with three bicycles lying on their sides in the lawn; the Lauchaires', where Mrs. Lauchaire was lugging a picnic table to the sidewalk for the lemonade stand she had promised Domi and Etienne; and the ladies' old house in the shadow of the Witch Tree.

Ellie was too far away to make out the face on the tree, but she could feel herself in its gaze, knew it was watching over the people in all the houses on the street. It would watch over Ellie for a long, long time. It would watch over her in seventh grade when she and Holly moved to the junior high, a bigger school where the sparrows held no power, and Ellie and Holly discovered that most kids couldn't care less what street their classmates lived on or what their mothers had done. It would watch over her during the long summer, one of the hottest on record in Spectacle, when Nan and Poppy came to visit, then brought Ellie, Albert, and Marie back to Baton for two wonderful weeks. It would watch over her that afternoon as she and her father would finally sit down with Albert and Marie and tell them the truth about Doris. And it was watching over her at that very moment as she heard the grinding of gears and turned to see the school bus pull up at the corner. The doors squeaked open, and out jumped first Allan, whooping and wearing a paper hat he had made in art class, then Marie, Domi, and Rachel, holding hands, then Etienne, craning his neck to see whether the picnic table had been set up, then Albert and David, yelling, "School's out! School's out!" even though one more day was left, and finally Holly, who waved to Ellie.

Ellie looked again at the Witch Tree at one end of the street, then at the kids at the other. In the space between was her whole life.